OF THE KNOWLEDGE OF GOOD AND EVIL

BOOK 2
IN THE
OPERATION: MIDDLE OF THE GARDEN SERIES

Micah Persell, author of *Of Eternal Life*

CRIMSON ROMANCE

F+W Media, Inc.

This edition published by
Crimson Romance
an imprint of F+W Media, Inc.
10151 Carver Road, Suite 200
Blue Ash, Ohio 45242

www.crimsonromance.com

Dedication

FOR CAMERON—

MY MR.

MY HAPPILY EVER AFTER

Acknowledgments

Eternal gratitude goes to Stoney-poo, my best friend, sounding board, and fixer of plot holes.

Thanks to Chatom for the book's ending and for calmly deflecting the panic of a writer who had felt she'd written a heroine too pig-headed for a happily ever after.

Thanks to Joyce, my storyline detective, for her sharp eye and flawless judgment.

Heaps of thanks to the beautiful Inés Saint and her wonderful friends Yvette and Leslie for giving up some of their girl time to help me with my Spanish. Any mistakes are, of course, all mine.

Thanks to Nathan, little brother, continuity genius, and father of the cutest nephew any girl could ever ask for.

And finally, double thanks to Carol Goff for her edits and to the incomparable Jennifer Lawler for all that she does, known and unknown, for the Crimson ladies.

The Lord God made all kinds of trees grow out of the ground—trees that were pleasing to the eye and good for food. In the middle of the garden were the tree of life and the tree of the knowledge of good and evil.

Genesis 2:9—10

After he drove the man out, he placed on the east side of the Garden of Eden cherubim and a flaming sword flashing back and forth to guard the way to the tree of life.

Genesis 3:24

Annual Report of Progress
from the Secret Files of Operation

Middle of the Garden

Close to nine years ago, troops in Afghanistan stumbled upon what was thought to be the Garden of Eden. They found two trees buried in centuries of sand. All five troops who discovered the trees were coerced into testing the fruit. Three troops disappeared forever and are presumed dead. Two troops were given the fruit from the Tree of Eternal Life, and it proved to turn them immortal. The fruit's use in modern warfare became a subject of heavy debate, and one Major Taylor was assigned the duty of testing the fruit further.

One of the subjects, Jericho Edwards, had a strong biological response to a female nurse: what came to be known as "Impulse-pairing." They exhibited symptoms not unlike those of animals with their mates. Unfortunately, the female became pregnant and died soon after conception. The female nurse was a civilian, and rumors of testing on humans caused the government to shut down Operation: Middle of the Garden. Edwards was returned to the general public; the other subject, Eli Johnson, was reported dead.

Eli Johnson showed up very much alive eight years later with an Impulse partner, now-prestigious geneticist Dr. Abilene Miller. Johnson reported that Major Taylor had continued secret testing on Johnson, and he was forced to kill Taylor to escape horrific conditions (see reports). Operation: Middle of the Garden was re-opened at Johnson's explicit request, and Johnson and one Sergeant Collins were placed in charge. Testing on the fruit of the Tree of the Knowledge of Good and Evil in conjunction with the fruit from the Tree of Eternal Life commenced, this time with volunteer test subjects: Jericho Edwards and Dahlia Gutierrez, Major Taylor's former assistant who is volunteering with the Operation to escape prison time for her role in Taylor's crimes.

Testing so far has proven inconclusive.

Chapter One

In her dreams, Dahlia was a free-range, castigating bitch. In real life?

Dahlia was an imprisoned, castigating bitch.

She sat with her back against the headboard. She rested her wrists on her bent knees and examined her nails with a critical eye. Beyond her nails, Dahlia caught a glimpse of her cell wall, and her relaxed lips quickly morphed into a grimace.

Three months she'd been a prisoner in this damn facility. Three months of being poked and prodded daily. And for what? A failed experiment that proved to turn her into some cosmic judge of character. Which was a freaking laugh riot, considering she was completely devoid of character herself.

But she wasn't in federal prison, and she had to remind herself often that all of this—testing both fruits; having to touch people over and over to determine if they were *good* or *evil*, an ability they'd termed the "Knowledge"; having to listen to their incessant talk of how the Knowledge would change espionage; being stuck in this terrible room—was worth it. They were lax on security here at the facility, and Dahlia never knew what life was going to throw at her, or when she was going to need to bail.

But—hand to God—she was going to kill someone if they forced her to touch and fruit-test one more do-good freak.

She heard a clatter at her cell door. Her head snapped up, and she watched through narrowed eyes as the door swung open and a man she hadn't seen before entered her cell.

Dahlia threw her head back and groaned to the ceiling. "God damn it. A new one?" She lowered her head and pinned him with a leer that had him squirming where he stood. "Is this really necessary, or are you just here so I'll touch you?"

Eli Johnson, bane of her existence and co-director of Operation: Middle of the Garden, entered the room behind the man who now looked like he faced a firing squad instead of one curvy Latina in a cell. "Knock it off, Dahlia," Eli said with a growl as he walked around his cohort. "He's not here for tests. He's here for—" He broke off to plow his fingers through his hair, and Dahlia silently congratulated herself for managing to stress him out with minimal effort. He was usually more unflappable than this. Today was looking up.

Eli took a deep breath, and then, "How are you finding your accommodations?"

For the first time in a long time, Dahlia grew wary. "Um . . . why?" she asked.

Eli shrugged. "We've been re-evaluating the conditions of your imprisonment. It's been suggested that you may enjoy visitation. Perhaps from friends. Or family."

Black ice filled her veins. "I don't have family."

They both looked at her for way longer than was comfortable, but Dahlia schooled her features into a mask. They could look all damn day. The answer wouldn't change. Not for them. Not for anyone.

"Okay," Eli said. "Just thought I'd ask." He then held his hand out, and the other man slapped an envelope into the open palm and then made a notation on the clipboard he carried. Eli strode forward and stopped right beside her bed. Dahlia realized she was holding her breath. "We had your mail forwarded here," he said.

Dahlia straightened.

"This came for you today." Eli dropped the envelope onto Dahlia's bed.

With measured slowness, Dahlia picked up the envelope, saw there was no return address, and turned it over. She cursed. "It's been opened," she accused. Rage flooded her.

Eli shrugged. "You're a prisoner."

As Dahlia saw red, Eli and the stranger left the cell. When the door clicked behind them, Dahlia tore the letter from the envelope.

One flick of her wrist, and it was open. The world tilted violently.

Ha pasado.

It's happened. The Spanish words blurred before her eyes as the letter fell to the floor. Blood drained from her face. She tried to pull air into her lungs, but her body wasn't cooperating.

Not this. Anything but this. Everything she'd done, all the people she'd hurt. Killed. She'd done everything to avoid this exact letter.

At the edge of hysteria, Dahlia managed to pull herself back. In the back of her mind, she'd always known this day would come. She would handle it. She would—

Her eyes flew to the door.

This was the reason she was here. Here and not in federal prison. Her eyes evaluated the riveted steel that separated her from the "good" folks. She strode to the door and kicked it with all her might. At the sight of her boot's imprint in the titanium steel, a grim smile spread her cheeks.

She drew back for another kick.

*

In his dreams, his Emily was alive. In real life?

Jericho was alone. Tormented by her memory.

The worst part was when he woke up, and for a few blissful moments, he didn't remember she was dead. He would roll over and reach for her, ready to pull her warm body into his own, and his hand would grasp air.

Just like it was doing right now.

The weight of his loss settled in on his heart, and Jericho squeezed his eyes shut tighter, prolonging the visual confirmation of Emily's absence a few moments longer. But the delay only caused horrific scenes to flicker against the black of his closed eyelids. The longing to sift his fingers through Emily's shoulder-length brown hair, to gaze into her large, expressive honey-colored eyes shifted as images of her sweat-soaked hair, screams of terror, and vacant eyes crowded happy memories to the back of his mind.

Jericho shook. The fruit forced his remembrances to maintain their perfect sensory detail. He could never forget her; his memories would never begin to fade.

And after eight years, he was ashamed to admit he wanted them to. He'd loved Emily with every fiber of his soul. He'd lived for her. He still lived for her, even though he'd been with Emily for only a handful of days.

He spent his time in equal parts grief, equal parts resentment that he couldn't shake the hold his mate had over him after the unfairly short amount of time they'd had together. If anyone had told him he'd spend eight years grieving his mate of only five days, he might have run screaming at his first sight of her.

Might have. Oh, who was he kidding. Nothing could have kept him from Emily. Nothing but death. A death he'd caused.

He'd give anything to set that guilt aside.

A resounding boom ricocheted through Jericho's room, pulling him from his thoughts. The picture frames on the wall shuddered and clacked. Jericho frowned and pulled himself to a sitting position, wondering if the noise had been dream or reality.

The boom sounded again, followed by a crash. Jericho's sleepy confusion evaporated. Something was happening. Apprehension settled into his gut.

Jericho walked to the door. Shouts bounced in the hallway, and for the first time since entering this room months ago, Jericho placed his hand on the doorknob. He took a deep breath and steeled himself to leave the solace of his room. He turned his wrist. The knob didn't budge.

Jericho frowned. His door was never locked. Granted, he hadn't tried it in all this time, but he had always known he was free to come and go as he pleased. He just didn't please.

The back of his neck tingled, and Jericho froze. The metal of the doorknob seemed to burn his hand. He brought his eyes up to the window of his door, and what he saw stole the breath from his lungs.

Eyes as dark as espresso. Smooth, luminous brown skin. Cascades of wavy, rich black hair. As he felt his own eyes widen in shock, hers did as well.

The One. She's yours.

The words stopped his heart. They were the same words he'd heard a mysterious Voice whisper eight years ago when he'd first laid eyes on Emily.

His body moved on its own to press against the door. The tips of his fingers skimmed over the cool metal on their way to the window, and his hand splayed on the glass.

Those beautiful eyes zeroed in on his hand, and her lips parted. Her brows drew together as she watched her own hand rise to meet his on the other side of the glass. His hand dwarfed hers—he couldn't even see it past his own fingers and wide palm—but he swore he could feel the heat of her skin through the barrier.

No, no, no. This couldn't be happening. He'd found—and lost—his mate. He didn't get another.

God, did he?

The weight of gloom lifted from his shoulders. Hope bubbled up through his chest, and he felt an unfamiliar pull at his cheeks. A quick check of his reflection in the glass showed he was smiling.

His heart started beating again in double time. He moved to try the doorknob once more, but before he could, he felt it turning against his palm and realized that he hadn't been able to open the door because she had been holding the knob in her grip. And now, she was coming in to him. His grin grew broader, and he refocused on her gorgeous features.

She stopped twisting the knob. Her dazed eyes grew sharp, and she jerked her palm from the window where it rested against his.

Jericho's grin slid from his face.

She bared her teeth at him and with a vicious twist of her

shoulders, the door screeched. She stepped back and held the mangled doorknob before her.

Jericho looked down to where his hand rested on his side of the knob and gave it a twist. It didn't budge. His eyes flew back to the window, and he couldn't prevent them from raking over her form. She was perfection. Tall. Curvaceous. Seductive. The hand he pressed against the window curled into a fist.

She sneered at him, dropping the knob from the tips of her fingers. He could hear the clunk as it hit the floor.

And then, with one final look of disgust, she turned her back on him and ran away.

Chapter Two

"Nope," Dahlia said as she jogged through the halls. "No, uh-uh, that did not just happen." She had not just Impulse-paired with that man.

That really, really beautiful man.

She could still feel those eyes all over her. *Those eyes.* So light blue they almost blended into the white, except for that brilliant, dark blue ring around his iris.

"Come on, Dahlia, he was blond," she scolded herself.

And delicious, her mind countered. Dahlia shivered and tried another turn-off. "And pasty."

Lickable. And tall.

She groaned. Things had just gotten complicated. Way more complicated than she was currently prepared to deal with. As if she didn't have enough to worry about. That letter had taken centuries off her everlasting life, and now she had Impulse-paired? She wouldn't be able to stay away from him. The draw to be near him—*with* him—would grow in strength until she was running toward him, begging him to take the pain away.

"Not good," she muttered as she jogged. "Not good, not good." Panic was sitting at the edges of her mind, waiting for her to let down her guard for a second so it could sweep in. She had to get out of here. Had to get home.

An alarm blared to life. She skidded to a stop and puffed out her breath. "Great." She heard the oncoming rush of booted feet and couldn't prevent a near-scream of frustration. She didn't have time for this.

Two young soldiers careened around the corner, spotted her, and picked up speed. Dahlia quickly scanned the hallway and found nothing useful. She spread her feet to evenly balance her weight and waited to see which one of them would actually engage her, and which would stall out because she was a woman.

As it turned out, they both stopped before her, their chests huffing. They looked at each other, clearly at a loss as to what to do next. The one on the left spoke first. "You need to return to your cell."

Her nerves at the fraying point, Dahlia resorted to her bitchery—the only thing she could think of to keep her sane right now. She nodded gravely and cocked her head to the side. "Make me."

The men eyed each other again, and then the one to the right reached forward and very gently grasped her left wrist while reaching for the restraints attached to his belt.

Dahlia rolled her eyes. "Men," she muttered. She stepped into the soldier's personal space, and he froze, making what came next even easier.

She thrust the heel of her right hand into the man's nose. He grunted as his eyes filled with tears, but he couldn't retaliate before Dahlia wrapped her leg around the back of both of his and elbowed him in the chest. He crashed to the floor, and she gave him a kick to the ribs that had him gasping and rolling to his side in an instinctive move to guard his vitals.

Now, the soldier on the left's hesitancy evaporated. He rushed her, and Dahlia pivoted to take the attack head-on. Her left forearm caught him in the throat as she jammed her right knee into his stomach. A few times.

When he joined the first soldier on the floor, Dahlia quickly snagged the zip tie from clenched fingers, and secured their right arms together. Neither tried to get up from the floor. They just looked at her with accusing eyes, as though she had betrayed the order of the world by being a violent woman.

Their censure didn't even blip on her radar. It was something she'd lived with her entire life, and it wasn't going to start bothering her now, especially when she had to get the hell out of here as soon as possible.

She turned and sprinted down the hallway, but only made it a few meters before she heard more footsteps charging her way. She sighed and waited for the onslaught. She'd just get through them as quickly as she could.

I'm coming, she mentally whispered across the miles that separated them. *I'm coming for you, baby.*

*

They were taking too long to get him out of here. Jericho paced the confines of his room for what felt like years before walking briskly to the far side of his room and charging the door. The boom that echoed through the room as the side of Jericho's body made contact with the door brought back the memory of the booms he'd heard just before *she* had appeared.

He dimly realized she must have broken out of a locked room similar to his. Was she another test subject?

The door flew from its hinges and across the hallway to strike the opposing wall with a clatter. Jericho spared just a brief glance at its twisted corpse before moving down the hall at a run. He passed several people but barely noticed their presence as he searched frantically for his Impulse mate.

Apparently, leaving his room after months of self-imposed imprisonment was a phenomenon worth noting. Those he passed stopped in their tracks and watched him with slack mouths. Jericho didn't pause in his search to address their silent questions.

He had to find her. Even though his instinct told him she was no longer in the building, he couldn't stem the instinctive need to search her out and confirm she wasn't here.

A hand fisted in the back of his shirt and pulled him to a halt. Jericho spun around without thinking and only just prevented himself from decking the now-shocked face of his best friend, Eli.

"Whoa, man," Eli said in a low voice. "Take a breath. Everything's okay."

Jericho realized his chest was billowing in and out, and he forced himself to at least exude calm.

Over Eli's shoulder, Jericho watched as Abilene waddled toward them as fast as she could, her belly swaying back and forth with her movements, her face flushed. As always happened when Jericho clapped eyes on the small blond woman, Jericho's chest constricted at the sight of her ripe body; everything he'd lost rushing back to the forefront. But it was different this time: the loss of his mate and his unborn child only a sharp sting instead of a devastating assault. Jericho frowned.

Abilene pushed Eli out of the way. Her eyes crinkled in concern, and she laid a hand on his arm. "What's wrong, Jericho?" she asked, just as the overwhelming Knowledge that she was *good* swept through his body—a result of the second fruit he was testing.

Jericho found that focusing on her words was difficult. His eyes wandered around the hallway, looking once more for the woman he had to see again.

Abilene crowded his front, her belly bumping him, and snapped her fingers in his face.

He forced his eyes back to her. "What?" He had to assuage her curiosity so he could get on with finding his woman.

He shuddered at the thought. *Another mate.* Never in a million years would he have guessed it was a possibility.

"Jericho!" He'd wandered again. Abilene was checking his pulse at his wrist, and Eli's look of shock had morphed into one of worry.

"What?" Jericho repeated.

"You're out of your room," Abilene said.

Jericho shook his head. He didn't have the mental energy to interpret the answer she needed to hear from him to let him go.

Abilene looked over her shoulder at Eli, who stepped up to help. "Jericho, buddy . . . you've never left your room before." He glanced down at Abilene, then flicked his glance over the growing crowd clogging the hallway. He leaned toward Jericho and lowered his voice. "And you're tearing through the halls like a bull in a china shop. We're . . . *concerned*."

This was wasting his time. "Where is she?"

Abilene and Eli looked at each other again. "Dahlia?" Eli asked after a beat.

Dahlia. Jericho closed his eyes at the sound of her name. It was as beautiful as the woman herself.

"You're looking for *Dahlia*?" Abilene asked, her voice cold. "That's what this is about?" Her dainty features hardened into a war mask. "What did she do to you? You can tell us. We'll send her away if we have to."

"No!" Jericho exclaimed before he could stop himself.

Both of them raised their eyebrows. Jericho stepped closer to Eli. "I have to find her."

His friend was obviously baffled. "Why?" he asked.

"She—" Jericho spread his hands wide. "She triggered the Impulse," he finished in a whisper.

Eli's brows crashed down over his eyes, his mouth formed a grim line. Abilene gasped and covered her mouth with her hand.

"No," she said. "Not her. Jericho, she's a terrible person. You have to be mistaken. You'd never mesh."

Eli simply asked, "Are you sure?"

Jericho thought for a moment. It had been just as it had been with Emily. The Voice whispering *The One* to him, the immediate feeling of connection, the drive to be with her in every way. Jericho shifted uncomfortably. God, he wasn't sure he was ready to feel that way about any other woman. But he was sure about one thing. Jericho nodded at Eli. "We Impulse-paired. I'm sure."

Eli clapped Jericho's shoulder. "Okay. Tell me what you need us to do."

Jericho blinked. He hadn't expected cooperation. He looked at the crowd in the hallway and shifted his weight back and forth between his feet several times.

Eli followed his gaze and groaned. "People, we have work to do. Determine how many were injured and if anyone has an indication of where she was headed."

"Injured?" Jericho asked as the onlookers dissipated.

"Yes, injured," Abilene said. "Dahlia left a trail of broken men in her wake when she escaped."

Jericho bit his bottom lip. That just didn't seem right. Anger flared. "What did they do to her to make her fight?" he demanded.

Abilene rolled her eyes, and Eli squeezed her shoulder. "They didn't do anything," he said. "That's just how Dahlia works."

Not possible. Jericho knew beyond a shadow of a doubt that he would not be paired with someone he wasn't compatible with. That's not how the Impulse worked. He only had to look at how perfect Emily had been for him to see that. Jericho could never love a violent woman; therefore, Dahlia couldn't be violent. There had to be some variable here that was still unknown. Eli and Abilene's prejudice against her was tainting their interpretation of the events.

Sergeant Collins, the co-director of Operation: Middle of the Garden, approached Eli. The older man walked right up to Eli and whispered in his ear, but Jericho was still able to hear every word. "Three men were admitted to the hospital. Four others were treated and released," Collins said. "It's bad, Eli. They're already forming a task force to retrieve her."

"That's not going to happen," Jericho interjected, jerking several sets of eyes to him. They were not going to run after her half-cocked and angry. "If you need her back, I'll retrieve her." That way he could make sure no one else hurt her or scared her into defending herself so vehemently.

Collins stared at him for several seconds, and then questioned Eli with his eyes.

"They Impulse-paired," Eli said.

Collins sucked in a breath. "Well, hell's fire."

Jericho was starting to get annoyed with the constant dramatic reactions. He may not have been ready for the pairing, but it had happened. Dahlia was his, end of story. He didn't appreciate hearing her maligned. "Call off your men, Sergeant," Jericho said. "I don't want her threatened again. You need her back, I'm volunteering to go get her. There's nothing to discuss."

Abilene sputtered. "You don't want *her* threatened?"

"Darlin'," Eli said into Abilene's hair. She huffed but didn't say any more.

Collins continued to measure Jericho with his eyes. After what felt like an eternity, the man clicked his tongue and said, "I can see you're determined. You can go get her. God knows you're trained enough to track anything. But I'm telling you, son," he wagged his finger, "you're on a schedule. I want to hear from you every six hours, and if you don't bring her back in two days, I'm sending out reinforcements. She's way too dangerous to have trolling the streets with civilians."

Jericho chose to ignore that last comment as he turned back toward his room. "I'm going to get a pack together. You can debrief me in thirty." He could feel three pairs of eyes burn his back as he made his exit.

Chapter Three

Dahlia gritted her teeth and pulled her "borrowed" hoodie further over her head, curling into herself as the police officers passed her on the sidewalk. She released her breath when they didn't look at her on their way around the corner.

Making her escape through the crowded streets of Washington, D.C., was less than ideal. She hadn't realized how close to civilization the lab was located, and it was damned inconvenient. She was moving way too slowly as she protected herself from being spotted.

Dahlia dodged wandering tourists while keeping an eye out for security cameras. They were everywhere. She knew how resourceful Major Taylor had been, and he had been flying under the radar of the government when he was testing Eli. The new Operation had complete government backing. They had access to everything, including the feed of any security camera in the country. And probably outside of it, too. Well, at least she wouldn't have to worry about those. She was headed to California, not London.

She spotted signs for an Amtrak station, and an idea formed in an instant. If she could get onto the train without getting caught by any security cameras, she had a decent chance of getting to Needles before getting recaptured. No one expected the bad guy to make her getaway on a train anymore, and she wouldn't have to worry about the hazards attached to stealing a car: Lo-Jack, fuel stops, nosy gas station clerks.

But a train ticket required money. No reason to risk discovery by hopping a train. Classic mistake. She had to go legit.

Time to steal some cash.

Luckily, this was a busy city, which meant a bank on every corner. After scouting the location of surveillance cameras, Dahlia propped herself up against a lamp post and watched the activity in a bank's lobby from the corner of her eyes. When a man who put a substantial stack of bills in his inside jacket pocket made his way toward the exit, Dahlia straightened, lowered her hood, fluffed her hair, and licked her lips. Show time.

The man was middle-aged and the best kind of victim: distracted. He was busy texting on a phone, one painfully slow letter at a time, as he came through the double glass doors, so he didn't see as Dahlia approached. She plowed into him, gasping as though surprised while quickly reaching into his jacket pocket to lift the cash. Then she stumbled back and pretended she was about to fall on her ass.

The man's reflexes kicked into gear, and he clasped her by both shoulders. His annoyance at being run into evaporated as his squinted eyes took in her long, wavy hair and exotic features. "Whoa there," he said with a wink. "Sorry about that."

Dahlia gave a breathy giggle. "Oh my goodness, I should watch where I'm going. Thank you so much for catching me." She even threw in a quick fanning of her face with one slim hand.

He released her and stepped back. Before he could continue what was sure to be some sort of inane pick-up attempt, Dahlia flashed him one more smile and then dashed off, giving the impression she was in a hurry.

Which she was. It was only a matter of time before he felt for his money. She didn't want to be around for that. She hustled around a corner and quickly checked her make. Five hundred dollars.

Thank God. She wouldn't have to rob someone else. This was enough for a train ticket. She peeked around the corner once more, saw her victim was nowhere in sight, and continued toward the Amtrak station.

She paid for a ticket to California and was waiting for the train just a few minutes later. She'd spotted several security cameras, so she was half hidden behind a pillar as she fumed that the train trip was going to take two days.

Two days! So much could go wrong in that amount of time. She needed to be there yesterday. Or last week. Dahlia sighed. Honestly, she should have been there for the last eight years. She had only herself to blame for this situation. Herself and all of her bad decisions.

As she was scanning the platform and assuring herself that the train trip was her best bet, she spied a young boy walking up to the edge to look at the rails. Dahlia forced her eyes away and stared blankly at a poster for the National Archives while she tried to swallow around the lump in her throat and ignore the pang in her heart. She only lasted a few heartbeats before her eyes were drawn back to the child, and then she jerked upright.

The little idiot was leaning far, far over the edge. Obviously, he hadn't studied gravity yet in school. Dahlia searched for a parent, but it appeared the boy was by himself. She took two quick steps forward before she remembered the security cameras.

Her eyes flicked to the closest one, and she breathed a sigh of relief that she hadn't walked into its line of sight. She glared at the boy's small back, hoping he would feel her stare and turn around.

He teetered, and Dahlia broke into a dead run. Just before he fell onto the tracks, she grabbed him by the back of his hoodie and jerked him backwards. He fell so hard on his bottom that he skidded a couple of times. Wide brown eyes blinked up at her like an owl, and his thin little-boy lips began to tremble.

She realized with a start that she was standing directly in the beam of the security camera. She stamped her foot and clucked her tongue as she turned on the boy. "Just what the hell did you think you were doing?"

*

"A murderer?" Jericho scoffed. "You seriously expect me to believe that?"

A muscle in Eli's jaw ticked. "I have personal experience with that fact, so, yes. Dahlia is a murderer."

Jericho fell silent. He didn't know exact details about Eli's torture, but he knew death had been involved. Repeated death. Because Eli had been a test subject for the fruit from the Tree of Eternal Life, he could never die. That knowledge had been gained by good old-fashioned lab work. Eli had been the lab rat.

If he said Dahlia was a murderer . . . "She conducted the experiments?" Jericho whispered, not sure how this conversation would affect Eli, and not sure if he was ready to hear the answer.

Abilene, Eli, and Sergeant Collins all exchanged a loaded glance. After several moments, Eli finally spoke. "Not personally."

A breath of relief. "Then you've never witnessed her actually commit a murder." Eli began to speak again, but Jericho cut him off. "Do you have proof?"

Abilene tossed her hands in the air. "Jericho, you can't be serious! She was working with Major Taylor! She personally shoved the fruit down my throat." When Jericho didn't say anything, she continued, "*After* she'd kidnapped me from Sergeant Collins's home in the dead of night."

Jericho nodded. "Yes, those are serious crimes—" and Jericho knew she would have a good explanation for behaving so poorly, "—but none of them are murder."

Sergeant Collins stepped forward as the tension in the room tripled. "All right, let's just take a break from this line of discussion. I *do* have some intel to share with you, Jericho." The man gestured to the long, mahogany table that dominated the meeting room, and all four of them took a seat while Collins continued. "As soon as Dahlia left the facility, I had a tap into every security camera in a one-hundred-mile radius. We got a hit about thirty minutes ago." Collins pulled the video feed up on his laptop, and everyone crowded close to watch the grainy footage.

On the small screen, Dahlia lunged forward and pulled a small child back from the edge of a train platform. A couple of seconds later, she began what looked to be a pretty heated lecture, and the child burst into tears.

Jericho gave the others a superior look as he felt an onrush of pride. His mate saving innocent lives.

Eli's lips twitched. "She pulled a small kid around by his neck."

"*Away* from the rails," Jericho pointed out.

Abilene pointed at the screen. "He's crying."

Jericho slashed his arm through the air, cutting her off, as another woman rushed onto the scene—the boy's mother—and put her arms around the boy, escorting him off-camera with a vicious, black look over her shoulder at Dahlia, who was surreptitiously glancing at the camera that had caught her heroic action.

Jericho fought disappointment. "She knows she was caught on camera." This was going to be a dead end. She wouldn't do anything he could use to find her if she knew she was being watched.

"Just wait," Sergeant Collins said.

A train pulled up to the platform, and they all watched as Dahlia visibly battled whether or not to board. They collectively sucked in a breath when, just before the doors closed, Dahlia jumped on board.

"Wow, she must be desperate," Abilene said.

Jericho silently agreed. Her choice to take the train had been a sloppy mistake. Whatever was waiting for her on the other end of her trip had to be pretty damn important.

"I knew it," Eli whispered and all eyes in the room turned to him. "She's got a secret. Her choice to take that train, even though she knows she's been spotted, proves how desperate she is to protect it." Eli turned to Jericho. Abilene and Sergeant Collins followed suit, and Jericho tilted his head, bracing himself for what was about to come. "Finding out what it is needs to be your main objective, Jericho."

A secret? Jericho knew instinctually that Eli was right, but what he was being asked to do—find it out and report it back . . .

"Why?" he heard himself ask in a defiant tone, which immediately got everyone's attention. Jericho was an order follower. Not once in his entire military career had he ever once questioned one of his orders.

Eli and Sergeant Collins looked at each other for a heavy moment, and Jericho fought not to apologize. But he needed to know. As his mate, Dahlia deserved a certain amount of loyalty—like all he had to give.

"Dahlia is . . . ," Sergeant Collins began, "difficult to manage."

Abilene snorted, and Eli dipped his head to hide what Jericho suspected was a smile.

Sergeant Collins shot them a look like they were misbehaving children, and then continued. "If we knew her vulnerability, she might be more willing to be cooperative." Jericho opened his mouth to argue—Dahlia's cooperation wasn't any of their concern—but Sergeant Collins cut him off. "And she may be hiding something that would be important to the Operation."

Jericho shut his open mouth. All argument evaporated, and shame rushed in. Of course they had a good reason for seeking out Dahlia's secret. And he had dared to question his superiors, to ponder defying orders. "Yes, of course," Jericho said in a quiet rush. "I'm sorry. Don't know what I was thinking."

"Thought and the Impulse don't really go hand-in-hand, man," Eli drawled with a half-smile that only made Jericho feel slightly better.

Sergeant Collins stepped forward and handed Jericho a folder. "The train she boarded will arrive in Chicago, Illinois, tomorrow, just before 0900. I have a chopper waiting on the roof to take you to the intercept point outlined in that folder." He clapped Jericho on the shoulder. "Bring her back, son. And stay strong. She's a tricky one."

Jericho gritted his teeth. The implication that he could be swayed from his objective stung all the more harshly because of the slip-up he'd just had in priorities moments ago. He was supposed to bring her back, he'd bring her back. He would allow nothing to stop him.

And then? Once he had himself and Dahlia back in the facility safe and sound? Jericho straightened. Well, then they could begin to explore what had happened to them the moment they'd laid eyes on each other. Maybe he didn't have to be miserable for the rest of his life. Maybe his instinct had paired him with another perfect mate: a sweet, innocent, loving woman who could make his life whole.

Jericho nodded curtly. "We'll be back. Expect us tomorrow evening."

Chapter Four

Dahlia sat back in her seat on the train and breathed easily for the first time in a while. The train had pulled away from the station over four hours ago. No one had stopped them, even after that little snafu with the security camera.

Trees zipped by the window, and Dahlia looked at the other passengers while trying to swallow down the panic and need to rush. The train car was fairly empty, which was why she had chosen it. Five passengers sat in various dove-gray pleather seats, all of them far away from her. She cringed at having to sit still for so long—she longed for action—but it wasn't like there was anything she could do. She was at the mercy of the general laws of time and space.

As the train turned a bend, a peculiar noise drifted in past the typical train-travel soundtrack. It took a few more seconds as the source neared for the other passengers to hear it, but once they did, they began looking questioningly at each other, their eyes clearly asking, "What is *that*?"

Dahlia knew what it was. "Son of a bitch," she muttered. She pushed to her feet and pressed against the nearest window, craning her eyes to the sky. She'd relaxed too soon. They had come for her.

A shiny, black helicopter was fast approaching the speeding train, and Dahlia wondered who was on it. Who was the person she was going to have to disable to get away? She sighed. Well, at least she was now distracted from the bulk of her anxiousness.

Her fellow passengers had begun to murmur to each other nervously. She didn't need them interfering. "Nothing to worry about. Looks like a military helicopter. They're probably running a training drill out of the nearby base," she told them with a confident stunner-smile.

There was no nearby base, but apparently, none of them knew that because all of them relaxed and resettled into their seats. The sound of the helicopter blades grew deafening, and Dahlia peeked out of the window again to watch the action.

A thin, black cord dropped from the cargo hold of the helicopter to rest of the roof of the car two behind Dahlia's. Moments later, a fatigue-clad, gladiator-sized man swung out of the chopper and began rappelling down the cord.

It was *him*.

Dahlia closed her eyes and gathered her strength as she tried to convince herself that it didn't matter who it was. She would disable him. He was nothing to her.

It only took her two seconds to realize she was fooling herself. She of all people knew the strength behind the Impulse. Thanks to biology and a lot of other mysterious shit, her body had claimed this man as her *mate*. Even now, as she watched the man descend closer and closer to the train, it was difficult to keep her eyes from eating him up. Her breathing was suddenly shallow and strained, and she had to clamp her lips shut to keep from licking them. Hurting him was going to be . . . problematical.

Okay, so you move to Plan B, a Voice coached her.

Dahlia nearly lost her footing. "No, not that," she said out loud, causing the other passengers to look at her curiously.

Dahlia closed her eyes and gripped the gray curtains. The Voice was speaking to her now? She hadn't heard from it since it had whispered *The One* to her back in the compound. The Voice had never spoken to her after she'd eaten the fruit from both trees, and she'd hoped that, maybe, she would be spared this particular side effect of the Impulse. She didn't particularly crave the presence of some kind of cosmic Jiminy Cricket. A benevolent guide would hinder her ability to wreak havoc without a thought. This situation was getting more and more inconvenient by the heartbeat.

Plan B? Dahlia had to admit, she needed one. She wouldn't let the fact that the idea had come from a stranger in her head lead her to make a stupid mistake.

The blond behemoth landed safely on the roof, and Dahlia knew it was time to move. She tore her eyes away from his mouth-watering form. A closet. She needed a closet or a small bathroom to hole up in. It would at least delay the inevitable confrontation and give her time to formulate a plan.

Dahlia turned and strode through the doors connecting to the next car. She hurried through three cars, putting more distance between herself and the man who had come for her before she finally spotted a small, locked door.

She waited until a couple of passengers passed her and left the car before she broke the lock with a twist of her hand and closed herself into the darkened supply closet. It was surprisingly roomy for its purpose. Dahlia wedged herself between a mop bucket and a broom resting against the far wall and slid to the ground. She drew her knees up to her chest and locked her arms around them while she forced her breathing to calm so she could think. She kept her eyes on the vent at the bottom of the door. She could see daylight through it, and so she would know when he'd found her because he would block the light.

She had moments—maybe a couple of minutes, tops—before show time. She found herself wishing she knew more about him so she would know the most effective tactic. She did have biology on her side, since they had Impulse-paired, he would want to please her, even if he didn't understand why. All she needed to do was come up with a convincing story.

Tell him the truth, the Voice said.

She snorted. That was *not* going to happen. She hadn't told this particular truth to anyone in eight years. She wasn't about to tell someone she didn't even know—someone who worked for the enemy.

But she *would* stick as close to the truth as possible. That was just Lying 101. She'd have an easier time remembering what she'd told him if it wasn't an outrageous fabrication.

And she had another weapon. One that had never let her down. Her whole life, men had valued her only for her looks. It was something she'd learned to use against them. Oh, she would get his compliance. It was as simple as batting her eyelashes. The man was toast. He'd never know what hit him.

And the fact that she was looking forward to seducing him more than she'd looked forward to anything in years did not alarm her. At all.

She heard his heavy tread seconds before she saw two booted feet plant themselves on the other side of the door through the vent. She braced for a violent entrance, covering her head with her arms in case anything went flying.

So, she felt like an absolute idiot when he simply opened the door. She peeked up at him through her crossed forearms and was disarmed by his crooked grin.

"Hi."

She dropped her arms. "Uh . . . hi."

He stepped into the closet and closed the door behind him, and Dahlia wondered where all the space went. Hadn't she just thought this was a roomy closet? His presence dominated the space, and his scent wafted over to her: a mix of clean sweat and something deliciously pheromoney.

A distracting thought came from out of nowhere. "I don't know your name," she blurted.

His head kicked back a notch, but after a couple of seconds, he spoke. "I'm Jericho." The deep gravel of his voice didn't surprise her. Someone his size had to have an incredible bass voice—it was just science. Length of vocal cords and all that. But she *was* surprised that his voice caused her belly to quiver. Unbidden, she imagined that rough voice breathing wicked words into her ear as he licked and nibbled his way up her neck.

A short sound burst from her throat, and Jericho startled and looked at her with concern. She had to get a grip! This was life or death, and she was fantasizing about him. It was damn embarrassing.

She had to clear her throat before anything would squeak past the lump lodged there. "Jericho," she whispered. "I need your help. I'm in trouble." Time for a small dose of truth. "There's a reason I had to leave the facility."

She could see him nod in the dim light. "I knew there had to be," he said.

She frowned at his confident tone. How could he know such a thing? Another man who thought he knew her. Annoyance sharpened her words. "If I get on that helicopter, it will cost someone their life," she spat at him.

Dahlia reeled back in shock. Holy hell. She'd just blurted that out! Yeah, she'd planned on sticking close to the truth, but what she'd just said *was* the truth—not close to. Dahlia fought the urge to slap her hand over her mouth.

Silence descended upon them in a thick blanket. She stiffened as he walked toward her and motioned for her to move over, and then he wedged his big body down next to hers on the floor.

He was overwhelming. The tantalizing scent that had caught her attention when he first entered the closet now rolled over her in waves. She squeezed her hands into fists, realizing in horror that she wanted to reach for him. Heat from his body scorched her, and she felt the need to fan herself.

He wasn't even touching her. He was sitting a respectful distance apart from her, as far as the confining space allowed, and she was ready to tear her clothes off. His too. She licked her lips as her imagination got away from her. Maybe his *first*.

"A statement like that deserves an explanation," he said. His voice had gotten impossibly deeper. It was obvious their proximity was not affecting just her.

Damn, they were in trouble.

She mentally shook herself. No, this was the reaction she wanted from him. She needed him to be putty in her hands. She just had to get a grip on herself, and then everything would be okay. Remembering her mission sobered her up pretty quickly.

She turned toward him in the dark. "I'll go back with you, Jericho," she purred at him, "I promise." That was never going to happen. "I just need to do something first." She took a deep breath. "Someone I . . . love . . . very much," she inwardly cursed as she felt actual—not manufactured—tears rise to her eyes, "is being threatened, and I have to help."

*

She's telling the truth, the Voice whispered. Jericho had to stop himself from nodding. Yeah, that was the feeling he was getting, too. Those tears weren't faked. She seemed embarrassed by them.

Someone she loved very much? A man? Jericho rubbed the ache in his chest. God, that thought *hurt*. The heat from her body was drawing him in as though it had its own gravitational pull. Sitting so close to her had been a mistake. He'd just been trying to put her at ease. Instead, he'd placed himself within touching distance, and *damn*, he wanted to touch. Did her hair feel as silky as it looked? What would it smell like if he buried his face in it?

It had been eight years since he'd touched a woman—eight years since Emily had died—and in all of that time, he'd never once looked in the direction of another woman. Emily had been the first woman he'd ever been with, and any desire for sex had died with his mate. Now he was feeling the strain of eight celibate years. His hands where they rested on his knees were shaking.

He was surprised and relieved that his attraction to Dahlia didn't feel like a betrayal. Despite what the others at the facility had told Jericho about Dahlia, she was now his mate. The Voice would not have chosen anyone less-than-perfect for him, just as Emily had been. His first mate had been an amazing, generous, understanding woman. And she would want Jericho to be happy.

"Jericho, please," Dahlia said, drawing him from his thoughts. "I know it's a lot to ask. You don't even know me. But I promise you, I won't be able to live with myself if anything happens to—" She stopped abruptly, and Jericho saw her shrug in the dark. Apparently, there was no more to say on the matter.

Jericho knew exactly how she felt. Not being able to live with himself had been the status quo since Emily's death. How many times had he relived their short lives together? Emily's death had been his fault. He had gotten her pregnant. It had been his baby that had drained the life from her, stealing her away from him in an impossibly short span of days. If only they had known that the fruit was what would kill her. And what could have saved her. Jericho's baby, strong from his immortal father, had taken more than Emily's body could afford as it grew. If they had known that would happen, they could have given her the fruit as well, and Jericho's life would not be hell right now. He'd have Emily. He'd have an eight-year-old child.

He'd have everything.

He heard a noise from Dahlia's side of the closet, and when he refocused, it was to find her face a hair's breadth from his own. He felt his mouth open slightly and heard his breath start to come more quickly. Maybe he *could* have everything. This time. Dahlia had eaten the fruit. If they ever started a family, his babies wouldn't kill her.

He got instantly drunk on the idea. His mate. His children. Oh, God, he wanted that.

He noticed dimly that Dahlia's breathing had sped up, too. He stopped thinking and just let the feeling of being close to her take him over. His eyes rolled back into his head. His fists unclenched and reached toward her.

"Please, Jericho," she whispered. The words blew across his lips. "I need your help."

And then she closed the remaining distance between them. He groaned aloud as her lips brushed his. His arms came up and dragged her to him, crushing her breasts against his chest as he pulled her into his lap. He felt the fruit from the Tree of the Knowledge of Good and Evil ready its verdict on her, and he prepared to ignore it. He already knew what it would say.

It rose up in his brain and breathed its answer throughout his soul: *EVIL*.

Chapter Five

Jericho shoved Dahlia away, and she landed in the corner with a clatter from the broom. As he scrambled to his feet, he heard her curse as he stepped on her hand, but he was too panicked to apologize.

Evil? She couldn't be evil. She was his mate! He could never love an evil person, and she had been paired with him; therefore, it had to be a mistake.

Dahlia got to her feet and walked toward where he was plastered against the door, and Jericho could feel himself cringe as she got closer.

"Jericho?"

He had to know for sure. When she stopped before him, he raised his hand and brushed his fingertips across her cheek. Just as she turned her face into his palm, the Knowledge spoke to him again: *evil*.

Jericho lurched away and bent double, hands on his knees. He clamped his teeth shut as his stomach tried to void everything he'd eaten that day. He saw Dahlia reach out her hand from the corner of his eye. "Don't touch me," he snapped.

She jerked her hand back, and then his thoughts, which had frozen, suddenly started rushing through his shocked mind.

They were right. Eli, Abilene, Sergeant Collins—everything they'd said about her . . . he realized now, they'd been *kind*. They'd been trying to protect his feelings. How obviously had he been besotted with this terrible person?

"Oh, God," he moaned. He'd been ready to leave Emily's memory behind. For *her*. He fell to his knees as the retching started again, and this time, he jerked the mop bucket toward himself just in the nick of time as he lost his breakfast.

I'm sorry, I'm sorry, I'm sorry. He sent the mantra heavenward, hoping Emily heard it. He knew Dahlia continued to call his name. Knew she expected him to capitulate to her plan. She probably expected him to melt in her hands. He was ashamed to say he had been headed there pretty quickly.

He forced his body back into his control. He wouldn't make this mistake again. He had orders, and now—thankfully—there was nothing to prevent him from fulfilling them wholeheartedly.

He could play along. Pretend to be her ally, then find out what her secret was. And then he would haul her ass right back to the facility, see that she was locked back in her cell, and he would begin forgetting her. Forever.

Decided, he straightened to his feet and silenced Dahlia's repetition of his name with a short "Shut up." He winced. That would not convince her he was on her side. He couldn't even bring himself to look at her, but he offered an apologetic grimace. It was the best he could manage, and he hoped it would stem off her suspicion.

He forced himself to meet her eyes and just prevented a flinch. "So," he said, forcing a carefree air, "Where are we going?"

*

Uh, what just happened? Dahlia thought to herself. *And why, God why, isn't he kissing me anymore?* Holy crap, had that been a life-changing experience. He'd tasted like heaven. His body had been firm and insisting against hers. And just when it had been getting good, he'd pushed her away.

Ah, yes. That would have been right around the time that she had gotten the *good* reading on Jericho from their skin contact. She narrowed her eyes as she looked at Jericho where he was slouched in the corner and avoiding her eyes. So, her man couldn't handle her wild side? Interesting.

And not at all painful.

She cleared her throat. "I need to go to California," she answered. That much information wouldn't hurt her. He didn't know where in California, and she wasn't going to tell him.

Nevertheless, Jericho straightened, crossed his arms over his barrel chest, and raised both eyebrows at her. Good, at least now he was intrigued.

California had a lot of history for the subjects involved in Operation: Middle of the Garden. It was where Eli had been held prisoner in a refurbished military facility. It was where Abilene had first seen Eli and Impulse-paired with him. It was where Eli had been killed one hundred forty times.

"California," he stated.

Dahlia nodded.

"Okay, then." She watched as he visibly struggled and then seemed to come to a decision. He shoved his fingers through his hair. "That's going to be a long trip," he announced abruptly. "I have information that at least three sleeper rooms are vacant on this train. Let's find one and rest until we arrive in Chicago tomorrow."

Despite reeling from the drastic change in conversation, Dahlia latched onto one thought: sleeper cars had beds . . . . "Works for me," Dahlia said. She headed for the door, and she couldn't help but notice how Jericho curled in on himself tighter to avoid being close to her. She rolled her eyes as she passed him. Out in the car, she turned. "You lead the way, big man. I'll follow."

He gave her a suspicious look and then left the closet and moved with purpose toward their destination. He apparently really did know where the vacant cars were. He stopped abruptly in front of a door, glanced both directions, and then pulled some lock-picking tools from a nifty kit in his back pocket.

Dahlia sighed, stepped around him, and broke the lock with a twist. She opened the door with a flourish and gestured him inside.

He glowered at her. "That's rather conspicuous, wouldn't you say?" he said, pointing at the bent doorknob.

"Whereas a jolly blond giant fiddling around with tools would absolutely escape the notice of the ticket-taker," she said, gesturing to the approaching employee through the windows of the connecting car.

"Right," he said as he quickly walked into the room.

Dahlia followed and shut the door behind her. Her gaze flickered over the room's interior. It was decorated in the same neutral grey as the seats in the other cars, but instead of chairs, two shelf-like beds were connected to opposite walls.

She gave Jericho's back the snake eye. Of course he'd taken them to a room with two beds. Couldn't make her job easier by taking them to a room with one cozy bed. He was impossible.

Jericho settled on the far bed where he could watch the door, so Dahlia sat on the remaining bed. It was time to play her trump card.

"You know there are side effects to Impulse-pairing, right?" she asked.

He stared at her and said nothing.

His glare was both uncomfortable and caused a flare of heat to travel up her spine. "What I mean is," she continued, "we're going to be compelled to be together physically." She laughed as though this were embarrassing. "And if we don't comply, our bodies will go through intense cycles of pain."

Jericho continued to stare.

"The most time ever recorded for abstinence is three da—"

Jericho erupted from his seat. "You think I don't know that?" he bellowed. "I was Subject One, you crazy woman. You have that information because you studied me! And my mate!"

Whoa. Damage control. "Well, technically, I have that information because of what we observed in Eli and Abilene." She tried a small smile. "I never observed you. That was before my time."

He scoffed. That distinction was apparently pointless.

"Look, it's inconvenient, I know. But, why not make the best of it if we're going to be forced into it eventually?" she said, infusing her voice with sultry heat. His eyes narrowed as though he didn't follow her meaning. "I could . . . help you if you, you know, help me?" she finished.

He laughed humorlessly and shook his head. "I will not be touching you."

Before she could stop herself, Dahlia cringed. *Ouch*. His casual rejection of her . . . *hurt*. She prepared to shrug and play it off, but his words had struck at an insecurity she didn't know she still had. "Fine! Bury your head in the sand," she snapped. "We'll just have to take care of ourselves. That's just fine by me."

Jericho blushed to the tips of his gorgeous, muscled body, but said nothing. Dahlia shot to her feet and stomped toward the bathroom. She slammed the door behind her.

Her reflection in the small mirror over the sink stunned her. She looked . . . *wounded*.

"Yikes, girl, get that armor back into place," she whispered to herself. Now was not the time to all of a sudden start caring what men thought about her again. She'd grown beyond that ages ago. Sometime around the summer her first boyfriend had taken her virginity in a five-minute session in the back of his car and then callously tossed her aside. Or maybe the seventh time a man had used her for her body and left without a word.

She put the lid to the toilet down and sank to its surface. She rested her face in her hands and tried to regulate her breathing. Her eyes stung as though tears were pricking the back of her eyelids. But that couldn't possibly be accurate. She was just suffering from a flood of hormones. Her damn body wanted that man in the next room. He'd rejected that, and now her body was traitorously lettings its feelings show.

It was just biology.

Minutes passed as she tried to convince herself Jericho was just a job she needed to complete. When she finally got herself back under wraps, she raised her head only to discover that sunlight was no longer shining through the tiny window in the corner.

Dahlia groaned. She'd been in here for a long time. Possibly an hour. *After* erupting at Jericho that they were going to "take care of themselves."

Well, serves him right. *I hope he's imagining me having a marathon of multiple orgasms!*

She splashed some water on her face, took a steeling breath, and opened the bathroom door. The lights in the room were off, but she could make out Jericho's dim form where he lay on his side on the bed. His back was to her. His broad, beautiful back. Dahlia's mouth went dry, and flares of small pain from the Impulse flared in the pit of her stomach. She bit back a groan on the off chance that he was faking sleep. No need for him to know she was already desperate for him.

She crossed the room and flopped on her bed and crossed her forearms over her eyes. *Go to sleep, go to sleep,* she coached herself. The sooner she fell asleep, the sooner it would be tomorrow, and the closer she would be to her goal.

After a few minutes, she cursed softly. Sleep was not going to happen. *Well, may as well plan for California.* She turned on her side and stared at Jericho's back while she thought out her next steps.

Chapter Six

Emily's pure laughter rang through the room, and just like it did every time his woman laughed, Jericho's heart skipped a beat.

Her head fell back, exposing her long, graceful neck, and Jericho's mouth went dry. "You're so beautiful," he whispered.

She heard him, and her laughter faded away. She met his eyes with a warm smile, and she got up from her seat to walk slowly around the dinner table. When she reached his chair, she settled herself into his lap and placed her arms around his neck. "Thank you," she whispered just before placing her lips over his.

Jericho's eyelids closed, and he gathered Emily closer to his chest as he deepened the kiss. He loved this woman so much. She was everything he'd ever hoped he would have and so much more than he deserved.

He pulled back from the kiss to tell her this, but she was no longer Emily.

Dahlia sat in his lap. Her face was so close to his that he could see the flecks of green in her dark brown eyes. Her breath fanned over his face, smelling of cinnamon.

"Hmmmm," she hummed from between closed lips. Her tongue slipped out to brush along her bottom lip, and he zeroed in on it like a hawk. "You taste so good," she murmured in her luscious, husky voice. "Kiss me again."

And, God help him, he did. His mouth crashed down on hers before he could stop himself, and he discovered that not only did she smell of cinnamon, she tasted of it, too. He moaned into her mouth as she sucked on his tongue, and something inside of him cracked.

He jerked Dahlia closer. She immediately shifted her legs so that she was straddling him, placing the hot epicenter of her body over the fly of his jeans. He jumped beneath her, and she ended the kiss to stare hotly into his eyes.

"I know exactly what you need, Jericho," she said, and then she rolled her hips, pressing herself against him. His body bucked into her on instinct; his hands fell to those incredible hips in an attempt to hold her still.

Something was wrong here. He shouldn't be doing this, he just couldn't remember the reason why. And what she was doing felt so good. He couldn't remember the last time he'd felt good. He needed this; he needed her.

And so, he hesitantly thrust against her. She dropped her head to his shoulder, placed an open-mouthed kiss to his neck, and whispered, "Just like that."

So he did it again. And again.

His body began to shake. Really hard. He frowned.

Jericho's eyes popped open to stare widely at the pillow his face was buried into. He was panting into the linen, and someone was shaking his shoulder with all their might.

And he was thrusting into the mattress with each one of his hoarse gasps.

"Jericho!" Dahlia said loudly, obviously not for the first time, as she sounded annoyed.

Reality came crashing in, and Jericho scrambled back from Dahlia's hand, only to hit his head on the wall with a thump. He cursed and shook his head to clear it. Thank God her hand had been on his t-shirt instead of his skin. He didn't feel like fighting his gag reflex on top of everything else because he'd been reminded of her evil nature again.

But then he remembered what he'd been dreaming about, and he had to fight not to be sick anyway. He glared at Dahlia where she stood beside his bed. Maybe she hadn't seen what his lower half had been up to while he'd dreamt.

"That was . . . some dream you must have been having," she said with a smirk.

Jericho sighed. So much for that pipe dream. "What I dream about is none of your business," he said. He cast a surreptitious glance at his lap to make sure he wasn't revealing any evidence that he hadn't yet fully shaken the dream. No such luck.

"Yeah, well, about that," she said slowly and in a tone Jericho didn't appreciate.

He returned his eyes to her and narrowed them in warning.

"If you're having a dream like *that*," she pointed delicately to his still-obvious erection, "then you obviously didn't handle things last night."

Jericho's mouth flopped open. Did the woman have no shame? There were so many things he wanted to say to her in response, but what slipped out was, "Do you mind not *pointing* at it, for God's sake?"

She smiled; Jericho winced. "Of course," she said lightly, returning her hand to her side. "Do you mind not screwing my mission because you're a *caco*?"

Whatever that was, it didn't sound good. "Excuse me?"

Dahlia's smile had disappeared. "This isn't a joke, Jericho. The pain from the Impulse is real. You don't take care of it, and it will overtake you. You'll become a liability I can't afford to have, and if you so much as delay me by a second, I'll drop your ass."

Jericho unfolded to his full height. "You'll drop my ass?" he asked. "How about I haul *your* ass back to the facility right now?" He realized his threat was impotent as soon as it left his mouth. He couldn't take her back until he'd figured out her secret.

He didn't know what he expected Dahlia to do in response, but stomp over to him and stand toe-to-toe while she stuck her finger in his face was not even close to on the list.

"Do it, *cabrón*. Then I can break out again and make sure no one follows next time." She suddenly smiled, making Jericho uneasy. "Everything you can do, baby, I can do better, so try it. See what happens."

He had nothing to say to that. And, unfortunately, she had a point about the Impulse. And since her mission was currently his mission as well . . . . . "I'll handle the Impulse," he said through gritted teeth. "You won't have to worry about me slowing you down."

He'd handle it, but there was no law that said he had to handle it *now*. He knew his own body—knew how much he could handle and when to cry uncle.

Yeah, right, his psyche taunted as Jericho noticed how enticingly Dahlia's breasts moved with her breathing.

Dahlia caught him staring and raised an eyebrow. Like a teenager caught red-handed, he jerked his eyes away, but not before his libido had him pondering if there was a way to screw her and not have to touch her.

The train began to slow, and Jericho breathed a sigh of relief as he was pulled from that destructive line of thought. He'd be able to get out of this bedroom, with its beds, cramped quarters, and insanely attractive, evil passenger.

"They gave you money, right?" Dahlia asked abruptly.

Jericho frowned. "Uhhhh . . . "

"Because if you're going to be this entertaining for the rest of the trip, I need a book to read," she tossed over her shoulder as she exited the room without waiting for him.

He followed quickly on her heels, not sure if she was going to try anything stupid. She had just threatened to, after all. Granted, he had threatened her first. "I think we can manage that," he said to her back as he tried to keep up.

She hopped down from the train onto the platform and kept up her pace as she spotted the gift shop. They had plenty of time until the connecting train, so she had to be hustling because she needed some space from him. He could definitely understand *that* particular need.

When they entered the store, Jericho took up residence against the wall and let Dahlia hit the book section without him. Let her have the illusion of freedom. He could keep just as good an eye on her from here as right next to her.

Nearly an hour later, when their free time had all but vanished and Jericho was fighting his body and the pain that was growing more pronounced with every second he didn't seek release, Jericho was preparing to go wrangle himself one criminal when she finally emerged with a hefty tome tucked under one arm.

"I'm ready," she said and walked past him toward the cash register.

Her cinnamon scent wafted over him as she passed, and Jericho bit back a moan. He caught a look at the cover. "Harry Potter?" he asked. Loudly. Everyone in the gift shop turned around and looked at him.

"That a problem?" Dahlia asked in a low voice.

"Um, no." As long as she let him read it when she was done. That looked like the seventh book; he hadn't read that one yet.

Jericho joined the end of the line while Dahlia marched right past him and up to the counter, bypassing the line of three customers who were already waiting. She dropped her book on the counter. The grumbling from the customers got the clerk to turn around from closing the previous order. The young Hispanic kid's mouth was open, ready to keep law and order in his shop, but then he laid eyes on Dahlia.

His mouth went slack for a fraction of a second, and then it slowly spread into a lecherous smile. He swaggered up to the counter, leaned on Dahlia's book, and stared straight down her shirt. "Anything else I can get for ya, mama?" he asked.

Jericho clenched his fists and was charging toward the counter before his brain had finished telling his legs to move. Dahlia's mouth was open to make her reply, but he cut her off. "Yeah, we'll take these," he ground out as he pulled a box of Clif bars across the counter. "For us to eat later. When we're together. 'Cause we're together."

What the fuck?

He could feel Dahlia staring him down, but he refused to look at her. He was too focused on what in the hell had possessed him to go primal all over the gift shop. He bet it had something to do with the fact that, even though he despised her, Jericho was aching to touch her body with every fiber of his. Literally aching. The pain was growing unbearable.

The clerk completed the order with clumsy fingers—apparently Jericho was doing a pretty good job of being terrifying—and handed the bag with his purchase to him without another wayward glance in Dahlia's direction. Jericho gently gripped Dahlia by the back of her arm, careful to make sure he only made contact with her t-shirt, and turned to escort her out of the gift shop while studiously ignoring the warmth of her flesh beneath the fabric.

She let him get as far as just outside the door before she jerked her arm from his grasp and snatched the bag from his hand. "Well, that was eye-opening, Tarzan. Wanna throw me over your shoulder and carry me to the train, too?"

He glowered at her. "Can you go anywhere without causing trouble?"

Her eyes flashed. "What would be the fun in that?"

He pinned her with a warning glare, and she remained blessedly quiet while Jericho purchased his train ticket. Then they were on the train. No sleeper cars this time. Definitely no sleeper cars. That dream was still too vivid in his mind.

Just as they both settled in to their seats, across from each other and next to a window, Dahlia opened her book and began to read. Within seconds, Jericho was bored. Damn, he'd been too busy keeping an eye on Dahlia to consider getting a book himself. Well, this was going to be an uncomfortable trip.

He reached for a Clif bar and pressed his head back against the seat as a wave of agony from the Impulse poured over him.

*

Jericho was fidgeting.

Out of the corner of her eye, Dahlia had been watching him shift back and forth in his seat for the past hour. She knew exactly what it meant. He was feeling the Impulse.

Damned, stubborn man. He should have listened to her last night. Then again, maybe she should have listened to herself. If he was feeling it, she would be soon as well. Observation so far had shown that the male always reacted to the Impulse more severely, but the female was always quick on his heels. She had a lot to look forward to. *Oh, goodie.*

Over the next several hours, an uncomfortable, itchy feeling began to seep into her limbs. She idly scratched her arm, her leg, her neck several times while trying to focus on her book. More often than not, the words blurred before her eyes as she longed to take sneak peeks at Jericho. She hadn't allowed herself to look at him under the unproven hypothesis that actually seeing him would make the Impulse worse. It sounded like a plausible theory. And so, she'd read about half of the final Harry Potter book without understanding a single word. Which only made her more irritable. She'd been looking forward to this book for a while.

Dahlia finally gave up and allowed herself to close her eyes for a little cat nap. She hadn't slept the night before, and she needed her energy for the next step in her plan. She set her infallible internal alarm clock to go off in a couple of hours and slid into a light slumber.

When she opened her eyes again, it was pitch black outside. Her first cognitive thought was that of need. She moaned softly as she shifted and pain shot up through her limbs. The Impulse was acting out in its full glory.

Shit. A quick glance at her watch showed her it was about midnight. Just perfect. It was show time, and instead of making a getaway, Dahlia wanted to straddle Jericho and go to town until she felt better.

She braced herself and glanced at the man. Her heart lurched. Damn but he was fine. He had fallen asleep, too. His head listed to the left, and his blond hair stuck out at all angles. He must have been running his fingers through it repeatedly. His mouth had fallen wide open, but even this didn't detract from his attractiveness. His face had softened in sleep, and he looked young, peaceful—

Edible. The irritation from the Impulse surged.

Dahlia grunted. She had to get a grip and get going. If she were away from him, maybe the pain would lessen?

Working off that thought, she glanced around the train car to make sure it was empty. It was: a good sign that luck was with her. She hefted the Harry Potter volume in her hand, weighing it and finding its balance point, before launching to her feet and braining Jericho on the side of his head with it.

She studiously ignored the devastation her action brought to the pit of her stomach as he made a soft sound in the back of his throat and then slumped down further into his seat. Out like a light, and without even a struggle.

That had been easy. Well, relatively so considering the action had made her feel about as bad as she'd ever felt in her life. And now she had to drag his rather substantial weight into a hiding place. She located a little nook behind the final bench in the train car. It wasn't perfect, but it wasn't far, so it won out over trying to find another supply closet.

She walked behind Jericho's chair, placed one hand on each of his shoulders and pushed quickly—before she could turn the contact into a caress. He slid to the floor. She walked around to his back, grabbed him under his armpits and began the long haul to the back of the car.

Overwhelming guilt niggled at her conscience as she dragged him across the filthy floor. Had there been another option? Any other way for her to get to her destination without anyone knowing?

She cursed. "Getting soft, *chica*?" she asked herself out loud. Other option or not, she had planned for this one. There was no time to regroup. And since when did violence bother her anyway? It was the most effective course of action, and she had a lot on her to-do list.

When she got Jericho to the nook behind the seats, she unlaced his boots and did a fairly decent job of hog-tying the man to the metal supports for the chairs. She stepped back and checked to make sure he wasn't visible to the casual passerby. Assured that she had done the best that she could, she strode to the emergency door, flung it open, and leapt out into the night.

Chapter Seven

Jericho's pounding head woke him from a dead sleep. He moaned as he opened his eyes and the light stabbed his retinas. He cranked his lids closed again. He waited a few moments, and then opened his eyelids once more, slowly this time.

He blinked several times to clear his vision, and still it took a while for him to comprehend that he was staring at a vivid display of chewed-up gum stuck to the bottom of a seat. He jerked back in disgust only to be brought up short by his wrists and ankles, which refused to move.

"What the—" He gave a tug and quickly found out that, yes, he was bound to the metal brackets of the seat with what appeared to be his own shoelaces. The fog cleared, and he snapped to attention.

"Dahlia?" he called cautiously. When she didn't answer, Jericho's temper snapped. "Damn it to hell!" he roared as he broke the shoelace holding his wrists with one powerful movement. He fumed out loud as he untied the impressive knot keeping his ankles immobile, and within seconds, he was free and storming around the car.

Nope, no Dahlia. But there *was* a partially read copy of Harry Potter resting in his old chair. Jericho brought his hand to his temple, felt a goose egg the size a seven-hundred-page boy wizard could cause, and cursed again.

"I'm going to kill her. With my bare hands." It didn't matter that it wouldn't stick. That just meant he'd get to do it again.

The emergency exit door was a wide open beacon, and Jericho stepped over to it and thrust his head out into the night air. The breeze the train created slapped him in the face, waking him further and clearing the last of his cobwebs. He eyed the embankment, saw that it would make for a soft-ish landing, and jumped.

As soon as he hit the ground, he tucked and rolled with his momentum. After bouncing and jolting over the terrain for what felt like hours, he stilled. He'd landed on his back, and he gasped up at the star-speckled sky as he pondered what in the world had led him to believe he was facing a soft-ish landing.

When he could breathe once more without passing out, he sat up slowly and took stock of his body. He was pretty banged up. He could feel bumps and bruises all over and there were some minor lacerations on his forearms from the desert brush. Also, he was pretty sure he'd hit a rock at some point with his elbow, which had swollen to grapefruit size. Luckily, the minor scratches were already beginning to heal. And as an added bonus, this new pain was pushing the pain of the Impulse to the side. Since he didn't have any time to waste, he dragged himself upright and began to hobble down the tracks. It wouldn't take long for his immortal body to heal itself. He would heal as he walked.

He forced a painful pace. Trains traveled at about seventy-nine miles per hour, so if he had been out for any length of time, she had a huge head start on him. He had to hoof it.

After about a half hour, Jericho had healed enough to move to a slow jog, and after forty-five minutes, he was sprinting across the desert despite the fact that he wasn't quite back to par. He found the point where she'd jumped after an hour, approximately ten miles from where he himself had jumped. So, he hadn't been out for too long.

His eyes trailed her path. Looked like she'd rolled farther than he had. He winced at the sight of blood in several spots, then dismissed the momentary concern with annoyance. He would not be feeling sorry for her.

Her trail was easy to follow. She hadn't been covering her tracks at all. Overconfident in her incapacitation of him, or did she just plain not care? She had set out across the desert toward the soft glow from a tiny town in the distance.

Keeping his eyes on her clear tracks to make sure he stayed on her trail, Jericho set off after the woman he was learning to hate.

The tracks got fresher and fresher—he was gaining on her—and when he entered the town after another hour, he estimated he was about fifteen minutes or so behind her.

He picked up the pace. Tracking her in an urban setting would be much more difficult than in the sand of the desert. By some stroke of luck, he spotted a blood pattern on the pavement and saw another one several feet away.

If she was still bleeding, she must have been hurt pretty badly. He was all healed up, and he'd hit pretty hard. Again, that concern flared, and again, he shoved it aside. That was just the Impulse rearing its ugly head. The only thing he felt for this woman was blind rage.

As he rounded the corner into a dark, dangerous neighborhood, he spied a figure limping down the street about a quarter of a mile away. Immediately, he knew it was her. He took off like a shot, his boots slapping the pavement as they flopped around loosely on his feet.

She heard him and looked over her shoulder. Even from a distance, he could see panic streak across her face. She shouted in alarm and put on a burst of speed herself, her limp causing her to list all over the road.

She was shouting in Spanish at the top of her lungs, and several neighbors came out onto the porches and watched the proceedings with varying expressions of boredom.

Dimly, Jericho realized that none of them were jumping to the aid of a woman being chased by a man, and wondered where in the hell Dahlia had taken them.

She cut across the overgrown lawn of a dilapidated house and tore the door out of the hands of an older Hispanic woman.

He could still hear Dahlia shouting as he followed in her footsteps past the wide-eyed homeowner clutching her faded floral nightgown to herself and standing where Dahlia had left her. He sprinted through the sorry excuse for a living room and rounded the corner into an empty bedroom, opening his mouth to yell at this woman who was causing him so much trouble and terrifying innocent people.

He skidded to a stop.

Dahlia was huddled on the ground in the corner of the bedroom. Her back was to him, and it was shaking with the force of her sobs, which echoed around the room. They were the most gut-wrenching sobs he'd ever heard, containing an entire world of sorrow, and they were so out-of-character that they drew Jericho up short.

A tiny hand appeared over Dahlia's shoulder and curled into her hair. Dahlia continued to sob and mutter in Spanish as a shock of black hair peeked up over her other shoulder. Below the hair, two bright, brown eyes peered at Jericho in interest. Those eyes widened, and the little head rose higher revealing a crooked smile without two front teeth.

Jericho's world tipped dangerously, and then the small boy spoke. "*¿Papá?*"

Jericho collapsed into the wall behind him.

*

Dahlia heard Gabriel whisper to the man who had been chasing her through the night, and she knew it was over. She'd failed at her one job in life.

She turned around slowly, so slowly, delaying the inevitable for as long as possible. She wondered what he would do as soon as she laid eyes on him. Would he shoot her? That was fine. She'd survive. But he was a vindictive bastard. What if he decided to shoot Gabriel? She nearly vomited at the thought.

She held her breath as she looked upon her attacker with dread. She gasped. It was . . . *Jericho*. Her sobs exploded again and grew in volume.

"Oh, thank God," she said between breaths. "I thought you

were—" She cut herself off just in time. There was no need to let everything out. Even she recognized that in the midst of her oxygen-flooded thoughts.

She dimly realized that Jericho looked green around the gills where he was slumped against the wall across the room. Gabriel tugged on her arm from the cocoon of her body, and she turned her eyes on him. She read the question in their warm depths. "*El no es tu padre, mijo*," she whispered to him.

His expression fell, and he looked at Jericho again. "You're not my dad?" he asked in soft, accented English.

Jericho shook his head, an expression of horror painting his features thunder-cloud gray. "No," he blurted. He looked at Dahlia. "What's—"

Going on? she finished for him mentally. Well, in at least this one thing, she was well and truly caught. "Meet Gabriel," she stated. Then she added defiantly: "My son."

"I'm eight!" he piped in cheerfully.

Jericho made a sound as though someone had punched him in the gut, and then he slipped to the floor.

Dahlia frowned just as Gabriel turned to her again. "*¿Esta enfermo?*" he asked.

Huh, there was a thought. Could the Impulse be affecting him? He certainly looked sick. "I don't know, baby," she told him. "Go see *abuelita, sí?*" She kissed his forehead and watched as he scampered out of the room, taking her heart with him. Panic flared that he was leaving her sight, but she calmed herself with the thought that she was here now. She wouldn't let anything bad happen to him.

Once her son was gone, Dahlia watched Jericho as he gulped air. If she didn't know any better, she would guess that the giant man was close to tears. It affected her in ways she didn't want to admit. The discomfort from the Impulse, which had been kept at bay by the adrenaline of her getaway, made a brief reappearance, and she found herself making her way to his side and sitting on the floor beside him.

He cast a fearful look at her from the corner of his eyes. "Your secret was an eight-year-old son. They never would have guessed."

"My *secret?*" she hissed, going from compassionate to pissed in the space of a heartbeat. "They sent you to find out my *secret?*" Dahlia closed her eyes for a second as waves of rage coursed through her. Of course, Jericho had only come with her to find out something to use against her. Didn't all men betray women this way?

She opened her eyes to find Jericho listing to the side, his eyes rolling back in his head. He threw out a hand to catch himself, and his fingers brushed against hers. She sucked in a breath at the contact just as the Knowledge whispered *good* to her. In that same moment, Jericho jerked his hand back, an obvious reaction to his own read-out from their touch. His wide eyes met hers in a panic.

She raised her brows. His reaction to her evil nature was beginning to bug her. He needed to get over it.

"I can't do this," he groaned, covering his face with both hands. Dahlia forced herself to contain her temper as his shoulders trembled. She needed to find out what the hell his orders were so she knew how to protect Gabriel.

Just as she opened her mouth to grill him, Jericho straightened and pinned her with a look so full of anguish that all thought fled. "It's done. My mission is done. I found out what they wanted me to. I can't stay here a minute longer, not around that—" He shook his head miserably.

Gabriel. He was talking about Gabriel. Why was her son affecting this man so greatly? *Of course.* Gabriel was the same age as Jericho's child would be if his mate hadn't died in pregnancy.

Before she could ponder that further, determination crossed his eyes. "My orders were to find out your secret and then take you back. We're leaving. Now," he said as he rose to his feet.

Dahlia saw spots as Jericho reached into one of his cargo pockets and withdrew handcuffs. He unceremoniously reached down and hauled her to her feet, turning her to face the wall and wrestling her arms behind her back. Her shock dissipated and she started moving, fighting with all of her strength to get free. "No," she whispered, panic mounting. He was so strong. He was going to take her away—away from her son—and she wouldn't be able to stop him. "No, you have to stop," she begged shamelessly, feeling tears rise up in her throat again. He didn't stop, and she felt the cold iron of the cuffs slap around her right wrist. "I have another!" she screamed desperately. "I have another secret!"

Finally something made a dent. She felt Jericho still behind her. Heard her billowing breaths echo through the room. They bordered on hysterical sobs. His heat left her back as he stepped away, and she turned around, pausing for a moment to wipe her wet cheek on her shoulder before facing him. His face was an emotionless mask; his light blue eyes were dark and lifeless, the pinch around them the only indication that he felt anything.

"You have another secret," he repeated without inflection.

Dahlia took a great, gulping breath and forced herself to portray a calm that was nothing close to how she felt. "Yes. I do. I'm willing to negotiate with information if you delay taking me back." She needed time—she didn't know how much—to prevent the worst thing that could ever happen to her. Jericho couldn't take her back, not yet, and if that meant she had to incriminate herself further, so be it.

Jericho stepped back even farther, obviously trying to distance himself from her. Was her emotion affecting him? She could only hope. "Start talking," he ground out.

Dahlia shook her head.

Jericho's expression turned even blacker. "Then we leave now," he said.

"No," she said quickly. "I only meant I won't tell you right now. Not before I have your word you won't take me back."

Jericho's nostrils flared. "I'm taking you back. That's non-negotiable."

The panic nearly overtook her again. "Please," she said

breathlessly. "I just need time. I will tell you everything you want to know—I promise—only, give me some time."

She watched as a muscle ticked in Jericho's jaw, and she allowed the smallest patch of hope that he was softening. "Please," she repeated.

He sighed, and she knew she had him. "A day," he grumbled. "I can give you a day."

Dahlia shook her head. "I need more. Five."

Jericho laughed without humor. "No fucking way." He examined her with a critical eye. "Three. I'll meet you in the middle. But this had better be the best damn secret intel I've ever heard, you understand me, woman?"

Dahlia held her breath. Three days. Would it be enough? It didn't matter. She knew she had pushed him as far as she dared. Jericho was on the edge. Asking again could get her hauled straight back to D.C., and that she just couldn't risk. She nodded.

Jericho acknowledged her nod with a grimace. "So spill."

"Not yet," she whispered.

Jericho growled and took a step forward.

"It's not something I can tell," she said quickly, holding up both hands. "It's something I have to show. And I will. Tomorrow morning. Just," Dahlia swallowed, "give me tonight with my son." Dahlia didn't trust him to keep his word. As soon as he knew the secret, there was nothing stopping him from taking her. She needed to delay as long as possible.

"I'm a man of my word," Jericho said sharply, guessing her doubt. "I said you'll have three days, so you'll have three days." He took another dangerous step forward. "But if you've lied to me—if there is no secret—I'm taking you back tomorrow if I have to pull you by your hair."

Dahlia stumbled from the room, one thought thumping through her brain: she had to see Gabriel. Had to hold him. She knew Jericho followed on her heels as she walked down the hall and into Gabriel's bedroom. She felt more than saw him stop at the door warily.

Esperanza was singing a lullaby to Dahlia's son in soft, dulcet tones. She spotted Dahlia, and then obviously Jericho behind her, because her wise eyes snapped with questions. In Spanish, Dahlia quickly explained that Jericho was a friend—she nearly choked on that lie—and would be staying with them tonight. Esperanza nodded and rose from the bed with a few creaks and a groan and motioned for Dahlia to take her place.

Dahlia lay down beside her son and gathered him into her arms, burying her nose in his still baby-soft hair. She rocked him back and forth slowly, and just when she was sure he had dropped off to sleep, he whispered, "Will you stay this time, Mommy?"

Her heart stuttered and she looked up to see Jericho still standing in the doorway. He stared at her and Gabriel for a few seconds, then turned and walked away.

Dahlia took a deep breath and returned her attention to her son and the hope in his eyes. More than anything in the world, she wanted to answer "yes." But she knew she couldn't make that promise. Yet.

Instead of answering, she shushed him gently and continued rocking him until his eyes drifted closed, and he fell asleep.

Chapter Eight

Jericho woke up to the sound of a child's laughter. As soon as he shook the strangle hold of sleep, his heart got sick. He remembered where he was and what had happened last night.

Dahlia had a son. A son the same age as Jericho's would have been if both his mate and his baby had survived.

He saw again the image of Dahlia forming a protective barrier between himself and her small boy, and his heart kicked. Last night, she had been . . . unexpected. If he didn't know any better, he would think she might have one or two redeeming qualities. And then when he'd touched her by accident—

The Impulse roiled through him, leaving flares of pain in its wake. It had jumped into the back seat of his subconscious when the adrenaline from yesterday's chase overshadowed it. No more, though. All of a sudden, Jericho needed to touch Dahlia again. More than he needed his next breath.

He shook his head and rolled to his knees. He didn't have time for this. His cell phone fell out of his pocket with his sudden movements, and he squeezed his eyes shut.

Shit. He'd forgotten to call in to headquarters every six hours like he'd promised. Just what in the hell was wrong with him? This woman was turning him inside out. He couldn't remember anything he was supposed to be doing. He picked up the phone and dialed Eli's office from memory.

Eli picked up before the first ring finished. "Jericho! Is that you?" Eli asked in a panic.

Jericho closed his eyes against the overwhelming feeling that he was an ass. "Yeah, it's me, Eli. Sorry I didn't call in sooner."

Eli let out all of his air, resulting in a loud noise over the phone. "Abilene's gonna skin you alive, man. What did you think you were doing? Did you catch up to Dahlia?"

Jericho opened his mouth to answer affirmatively and let Eli know Jericho had at least one of Dahlia's secrets and the promise of another, but nothing came out. He frowned. This was the part where he needed to tell Eli that Dahlia had a son—information that would ensure she was easy to handle and manipulate in the future. It was as easy as saying the words.

The silence on the phone grew uncomfortable. After several heartbeats, Jericho heard himself saying, "She's secured, but I don't have any intel to share yet."

What the hell? He'd just *lied*. To his friend. And why did he get the feeling that the Voice was pleased with his protection of Dahlia?

There was a pregnant pause on Eli's end of the conversation. Jericho fidgeted, sure any second he would be found out. "Jericho," Eli said slowly. "I want to warn you that the Impulse is very strong. I know you already know this, but when you experienced it the first time, with Emily—" His friend cursed on the other end of the phone. "Dahlia's not Emily, Jericho. That's all I wanted to say."

Jericho gritted his teeth. "I know exactly who Dahlia is, don't worry about that." Even as he said it, his brain flashed back and forth between the first time he'd touched her, finding out she was evil, and last night. "I also know what my mission is." *Did he?* "You know the type of person *I* am. I'll follow orders."

"All right, all right," Eli said in a tone of voice that made Jericho feel even sicker. "I didn't mean to insult your honor. We all know that if you say you're going to do something, you'll do it."

Jericho eyes slid closed. Yep, that was the reputation he'd cultivated for himself. He was proud of it. So why was he lying to his friend and delaying his mission?

"You'll call in more frequently?" Eli asked hesitantly.

Jericho made an affirmative noise.

"Okay, then. Just . . . be careful out there, okay?"

Jericho hung up before Eli could say anything else. His curse ricocheted around the empty room. "What *am* I doing?" he asked himself out loud. He should be dragging Dahlia back to the facility by her hair right this second. She was a dangerous criminal, the fruit had confirmed that. Last night, when he'd brushed her hand, *had* to have been a fluke.

A life-changing aroma drifted through the door, interrupting his self-recriminations. His stomach rumbled, reminding him that he hadn't taken time out to eat since the train yesterday. He stuck his head out into the hallway and looked left and right before following his nose.

When he arrived at the kitchen, Dahlia's son, he thought he remembered her saying his name was Gabriel, was sitting at the breakfast table watching the older woman cook at the stove. The family resemblance between the two was startling, which, Jericho reasoned, had to make the woman Gabriel's grandmother.

She gave Jericho a big toothy grin from where she stood over a skillet. Jericho smiled back uncertainly, not sure why she was being nice to him when he was here to take Dahlia away.

"*¿Quieres huevos rancheros?*" she asked.

Jericho felt his smile fall away. He shook his head once. "I'm sorry . . . I don't—" He shrugged.

"She's asking if you want eggs," Gabriel said from the table.

Jericho turned his attention to the small boy.

"And, by the way, you do. Grandma's *huevos rancheros* are awesome."

Jericho nodded at the woman. "Uh, *sí . . . por favor.*"

Her smile widened at his poor attempt at Spanish, and she gestured for him to sit at the table. Jericho shuffled over and took the seat farthest from the child. He studiously avoided eye contact, even though he could feel Gabriel's eyes boring into him with unspoken questions.

Gabriel's grandmother sat a steaming plate in front of him. His mouth watered at the sight of tortillas piled with fried eggs and warm salsa. "Thank you. I mean *gracias*," he said.

She nodded again, and patted his hand with her own. The Knowledge immediately responded with a warm *good*, and Jericho smiled genuinely at her.

He ate in strained silence until he could ignore Gabriel's eyes no longer. He braced himself and met the young boy's stare.

It was all the kid had been waiting for. "Are you my mommy's boyfriend?"

Jericho choked on his eggs. After grabbing a glass of water and clearing his throat, he discovered that both Gabriel and his grandmother were looking at him expectantly, an indication that the woman understood at least a little English.

"Uhh—" Jericho began.

"What do you know about boyfriends and girlfriends?" Dahlia asked from the doorway.

All three of their heads swiveled around to look at her. Jericho's breath abandoned him again as he laid his eyes on her. She was smiling at Gabriel in a way that betrayed she was head-over-heels in love with the boy. It made her stunningly beautiful. The Impulse shivered through him again, and he rubbed the palms that itched to touch her against his thighs.

Gabriel blushed and quickly said, "Nothin'."

"Um-hmm, that's what I thought." She winked conspiratorially at the other woman, and then motioned Gabriel to herself. "Come here, *mijo*. Give me *un beso*. It's time for school."

"*Ay, mamá*, you just got back!" Gabriel protested while clutching the sides of his chair as though one of the adults in the room were going to pry him from his seat.

Dahlia shushed him quietly and motioned one more time for her son to come to her. Gabriel pouted, but left his seat and dragged his feet over to his mother where he obediently gave her a peck on her cheek.

"I'll be here when you get back, baby," she said softly while pinning Jericho with a glare above Gabriel's head. He fought the urge to squirm.

Gabriel left the kitchen with a hanging head, and Jericho's heart panged as he watched Dahlia come into the room and take a seat across from him at the table. Gabriel's grandmother sat a plate in front of her, and she turned grateful eyes toward the older woman. "*Gracias*, Esperanza."

Esperanza. Jericho filed the woman's name away while simultaneously pondering why Dahlia would call her mother by her first name. Unless . . .

He looked at the women closely. No family resemblance. He frowned.

Esperanza kissed the top of Dahlia's head and then left the room. Jericho became instantly and acutely aware that he was alone with his Impulse mate again. Unbidden, his mind wandered down the hall and to the pallet he'd made in the floor of the empty room. Plenty of room to roll around . . .

Jericho straightened in his seat and shifted uncomfortably to lessen the pressure behind his fly.

Dahlia was eating quickly and neatly, and she was blatantly ignoring him.

It gave Jericho a chance to study her without interruption. What *was* he going to do with her? The obvious answer was take her back to the compound. That was his job. Those were his orders. But he couldn't risk the valuable information she promised. That is, if she wasn't lying through her teeth.

This would be so much easier if he just knew for sure she was evil. *Why* did last night have to happen? He cleared his throat. "So . . . " Dahlia didn't break stride in her eating. He tried again. "Last night, when I . . . touched you—"

Dahlia's head snapped up.

"By accident," Jericho clarified in a rush. He couldn't prevent a wince at her smirk. "Anyway, when my fingers touched your hand," he shrugged in an attempt at nonchalance, "the Knowledge told me you were . . . *good.*"

Dahlia stopped chewing. Her brows crashed down over her incredible eyes, and she tilted her head.

Jericho waited several seconds, hoping for . . . God, he didn't know whether he wanted her to confirm that she was evil or just the opposite. His brain was so muddled from her presence in the room.

When she just continued to stare at him, Jericho grew frustrated. "Well, which are you, Dahlia," he snapped. "Good or evil? The fruit's told me both, and it's confusing the hell out of me."

She rolled her eyes. "Sorry to be such an inconvenience." She went back to her breakfast.

Jericho made a noise of distress once he figured out she wasn't going to answer his question.

She sighed. "It's my opinion that evil is what you do, not who you are," she said slowly, as though talking to an idiot.

Jericho frowned. That made . . . sense. Testing on the fruit so far was inconclusive. They knew that each time a test subject had skin contact with someone, something whispered *good* or *evil.* But they hadn't run enough tests to know if the Knowledge was telling them if the *person* was good or evil or their intentions. Dahlia's hypothesis fit the findings.

He felt like growling. Why the hell did he have to make this discovery outside of a lab and in a pressing situation? If he didn't know if she was good or evil, how did he know he was doing the right thing by taking her back? He didn't know enough of her history to know if she was really a murderer or not.

Her jaw had started moving again as she continued to chew her food, and before he knew it, his eyes were riveted to her moist lips. Her tongue darted out to lick her bottom lip, and then she lifted another fork full of food to her mouth. Her eyes closed in bliss as she slid the fork between her lips.

Jericho bit back a groan at the same time he came up with a brilliant idea. He could touch her again. He could touch her thousands of times. And then he could average the *good* and *evil* reads until he had an idea of where she stood. His palms were sliding across the table to her side before he realized he was a freaking idiot.

"I have to take you back," he blurted. The sensual haze clouding his mind evaporated instantly.

Dahlia didn't argue. She just got a look of steel in her eyes. "That wasn't the deal. I won't leave him without a fight."

Jericho floundered. Something inside of him refused to drag this woman away from her child. What made it worse was Jericho desperately wanted to be in her situation: with a living son to fight for.

He straightened as he remembered her earliest attempt to persuade him against his mission. "Is *he* your life-or-death situation?" Maybe she hadn't been shoveling him a steaming pile of bull in that train closet.

Dahlia averted her eyes and shifted in her seat, but she didn't answer him. Which, in a way, was its own answer. An answer that might change things.

Help her, the Voice whispered to him.

Jericho did his best not to react, but the unexpected intercession of the Voice jolted him. The Voice had never led him wrong before, not for over eight years. He looked at Dahlia again. She hadn't moved in her silent challenge of him, and he had to admire her for it. She just sat there resolute. He wouldn't move her without hurting her, and even the passing thought of putting his hands on her in violence made him sick.

But in the end, he couldn't forget his orders. His job. And her nature. He was sliding down a slippery slope with this woman.

He shook his head at her. Fine. He would find out this other information, and then he would be taking her back immediately, promise or not—it was the only decision he could make and still know who he was. He watched as her eyes got even more flinty. Jericho swallowed past the sick feeling in his throat. Why didn't he feel like he was making the right decision?

Dahlia nodded at him once and then got up from the table to take her empty breakfast plate to the sink. Jericho stared at his own empty plate for a second before picking it up and following her lead.

He wasn't watching where he was going, but he heard when she stumbled and his head shot up just in time to watch her take a catching step forward while stifling a moan. Immediately, he knew it was the Impulse. They'd ignored it for as long as it would allow, and now it was demanding attention.

The plate she was carrying clattered to the floor, and, working purely off instinct, Jericho tossed his to the counter just in time to catch her by the elbow as her knees failed her. Thought fled. His fingers dug into her soft skin as the overwhelming Knowledge that she was *good* rolled through him. And then the tingles, the uncomfortable aches he'd experienced since waking this morning, receded. It felt so good to touch her that he moved around to her front and gripped her other elbow. Her scent wafted up, and he felt himself sway toward her.

"Are you all right?" he asked in a low, rumbling voice he barely recognized.

"No," she moaned, raising her eyes to meet his with an accusatory stare. "You touched me! Damn it, why did you have to touch me, you gigantic idiot?"

They'd just argued over what Dahlia probably defined as a deal-breaker, and yet Jericho could *feel* the connection between them growing stronger with every second his hands were on her flesh. He couldn't pull away from her if his life depended on it.

Though her eyes still accused him, she was apparently feeling the same, because she leaned forward, the tips of her breasts brushing against his torso and then coming into full contact as she stepped into his body, fusing them from knee to where her head rested against his broad chest. A sigh left her body on a shudder and her arms came around him, her hands pressed splayed into his back.

"I don't want this," she mumbled into the cotton of his t-shirt. "I despise you. You're going to take me away from my son."

He could only make a sound of assent in the back of his throat as his arms came around her body of their own volition. He couldn't deny what she was saying.

"So, stop this," she pleaded. Her arms tightened around him contrarily. "Step away from me and don't ever touch me again."

He tried. Or, God help him, he at least thought about trying. His body wouldn't obey. "I can't," he breathed. His breath ruffled her hair, and she raised her head to look at him, locking eyes with him and dooming them both.

"Then kiss me," she whispered.

He was moving to obey in the next breath. Her eyes slid closed the closer his lips got to hers. When he brushed his mouth across hers, her lips parted and she sighed into his mouth. His arms cinched tighter, molding her body to his. He felt her hardened nipples through the thin cloth of her shirt. Felt them push into his ribs even farther as she moved her arms, winding them around his neck and pulling him in for another kiss.

This time, when their lips met, she sucked his lower lip into her mouth and bit down on it. Hard.

He knew she meant to punish him for the threat he was to her happiness, but it unleashed something in him he couldn't control. An inhuman noise ripped from Jericho's gut, and his hands descended on her ass, grabbing roughly and hauling her up. He forced her legs to wrap around his waist as he charged forward. His knees met the cabinets with a crash and his knuckles scraped across the corner of the countertop as Dalia's ass landed on the pock-marked Formica.

The pain shooting up and down his shins brought him back to reality. He wrenched his hands from underneath Dahlia and jerked back. "I'm sorry," he blurted. Dear God, he'd been really rough. He could have hurt her. His stomach dropped. Maybe he *had* hurt her.

Before he could step completely from the warm shelter of her thighs, Dahlia grabbed his shirt and hauled him back in with surprising strength. "Don't you dare stop," she growled at him.

He frowned, his lust-fogged mind not understanding her request. "Please tell me I didn't hurt you," he said, grasping her head with both hands, his fingers tunneling through her hair, feeling for a bump in case he'd hit her head against the cabinet doors behind her.

Her head lolled back with his touch, and she moaned.

Jericho's fingers stilled, and her eyes opened to meet his. Her pupils were completely dilated. Her brows drew together as she gazed at him, and she licked her bottom lip, leaving it glossy. "If you don't kiss me again," she said, "*I'm* going to hurt *you*."

Jericho drew back, sure he'd misunderstood. But after a couple of seconds of staring at her mouth, he didn't care if he'd misunderstood or not. He moved in to close the distance between them again, and she met him more than halfway.

He tried to be gentle this time, he really did, but as soon as their lips touched, he lost himself again, seeming to snap. Their teeth clashed together, and he crowded into her further.

She was all frenzied movement in his arms, and he had a hard time keeping hold of her. Her hands roved from his back to his neck and into his hair until finally trailing down his back and clutching his ass.

His body jerked at the contact, and she used the movement to pull him closer to her, placing his erection directly in the cleft of her thighs. They both broke the kiss to suck in a startled breath.

Her eyes were devoid of their anger now, but in its place was pure wickedness. She rolled her hips, stroking him where he throbbed, and he fell forward, resting his forehead on the cabinet beside her head with a thunk.

He distantly realized he was thrusting against her, but he couldn't stop himself. Instead, he gathered her in closer, lifting with his hands beneath her ass again and moving her entire body with his frantic movements.

She gasped into his ear with each thrust, her breaths growing louder. "Touch me," she panted.

Jericho *was* touching her, so he didn't slow down for a few more frantic thrusts, until he realized that she would only ask if she wanted him to touch her *differently*. That brought things to a screeching halt.

He stilled and pulled back slightly. They were both breathing heavily, their breaths fanning across each other's faces. "Touch you?" he asked warily.

She nodded frantically, not sensing his change in mood as she wriggled against him to continue the movement.

Jericho closed his eyes. *Touch me.* He didn't know how. He'd been so young and busy climbing rank when he'd first Impulse-paired. Emily had been his first. And his last. And their short time together, little more than a few days, had afforded him little on-the-job training.

Dahlia finally noticed his reticence. Her head tilted to the side; her frantic breathing slowing slightly.

"I'm sorry," he mumbled. "This was a bad idea. Let's stick with our first plan. We can just . . . take care of ourselves."

"Hell no, we won't do that," she snorted. "You started this, you're going to finish it." And with that, she grabbed his right hand and placed it directly between her thighs.

Jericho groaned. She was *hot*. The heat from her center nearly scorched his hand through the fabric of her pants, but rather than pulling away, he melded his hand to the curve of her mound and leaned forward again, closing his eyes and breathing in the waft of her scent.

Oh, God, he was so screwed.

*

Dahlia was smack-dab in the middle of the most exciting sexual experience of her life, and now *he* was throwing on the brakes?

Loco, she thought. There was no way she was letting him off the hook. From the second he'd picked her up and charged across the kitchen with her, Dahlia had been on the edge of the most powerful orgasm she had yet to experience.

Jericho, Mr. Play-by-the-Rules-and-Follow-Orders, was the most aggressive, out-of-control man she'd ever kissed. He'd surprised the hell out her with his rough thrusts and man-handling. And if he didn't finish her, she was going to quite possibly die on the spot.

His hand was a brand against the center of her body where she'd placed it. She could feel her arms shaking where they were propped against the countertop, holding her up. He was definitely affected—he'd slumped forward again, their chests touching, his breath tickling her behind her ear, his shoulders trembling—and yet, he still wasn't moving his hand.

"Jericho, if you don't do something, *anything*—" She didn't get to finish her statement, because she was cut off by the sharp nip of his teeth on her ear.

"I don't know what I'm doing," he whispered softly, so softly Dahlia was sure she must have misunderstood.

She jerked back to meet his eyes, and, yup, he was avoiding meeting hers, staring intently at a spot over her shoulder. And, yet, he *still* had to be kidding. Didn't know what he was doing? After being so forceful and take-charge mere minutes ago? "Trust me," she whispered back, "You know what you're doing."

She placed her hand over his and applied pressure. Pleasure rocketed through her, and she gasped, bringing Jericho's eyes to hers again with an almost audible snap. Lust flared brightly in those otherworldly blue eyes, but Dahlia was unable to relax in her triumph. The simple pressure of their hands had strung her too tightly.

He made a tentative movement with his thumb, circling gently, and Dahlia's hand fell away while her back arched.

"Mmmm," she hummed in encouragement, and so he did it again. Her hands flew to his arms, clinching his biceps, and he picked up a steady rhythm.

"You're wet," he gritted. "I can feel it through your pants."

"Because I need you so bad," Dahlia said, though it sounded like a garbled *Ugh* through the roaring in her ears.

And just like that, Jericho was right back to where he'd been before he'd gotten self-conscious. His tentativeness vanished, and he took control. His thumb grew firmer, and he rotated his hand so that he was cupping her more completely.

His other hand rose to her jaw, and he tipped her head far back, his lips descending on hers in a crush. He didn't ask permission; his firm lips pried hers open, and his tongue filled her mouth, rubbing against her own in delicious swirls.

Dahlia knew she was continuously moaning, but she couldn't stop herself. Damn, but this man knew what he was doing. His skin was so hot where her hands clutched him, and if the Knowledge was telling her he was good or bad, she couldn't hear it over the demands of her body.

The hand under her jaw vanished, and Dahlia felt him grasping her right wrist. He guided her hand to the front of his pants and planted it there roughly.

Her fingers immediately curled around the impressive erection behind his fly, and he made a desperate sound in the back of his throat at the same time that his hips twitched, surging into her grip.

His kiss grew more frantic, his fingers tripping over the folds of fabric to tug at her button fly. "Buttons?" he accused when he briefly drew back from the kiss to pin her with a glare. Before she could answer, his lips covered hers again, then moved to the corner of her mouth, her cheek, her jaw, her neck.

"Oh, God," Dahlia groaned, leaning her head back and giving him more direct access to her neck.

And then his fingers delved under the fabric of her panties.

She froze, her nails imbedded in the skin of his arm, certain she was going to come just from this touch.

"*Dahlia*," he groaned, nipping her collarbone. "What are you doing to me?" He sounded mildly distressed. Because he was out of control? He certainly seemed out of control to *her*. Not that she was complaining.

Her own fingers fumbled with his fly, and after getting the zipper down, she was finally able to wrap her fingers around him skin-to-skin. His entire body shuddered; his fingers trembled against her opening. All of a sudden, *What are you doing to me?* didn't seem like such an oddball question. He was huge in her hand. She could feel his racing pulse against her palm, and he was continuing to harden. He was bigger than any man she'd ever been with, and the twitching of his erection was testament to how affected he was.

It was apparent that his reaction to her was freaking him out. Yeah, well, this situation wasn't normal for her either, but it was the best thing she'd felt in years.

He slid one, and then two of his thick fingers inside her body, barely pausing between, and then he resumed the steady pace with his thumb, circling her clit in firm, sure movements.

She started to move, too. She tightened her grip and moved her hand up and down his substantial length. Every time she reached the tip and made the journey back down to the base, Jericho made a harsh, guttural noise.

Soon their hands were moving quickly, their panting breaths ricocheting around the kitchen.

Jericho drew back from kissing and biting her shoulder to stare into her eyes. "You *will* come first," he demanded of her, almost desperately as her fingers encountered a weeping tear at the tip of his erection.

And just as though her body had answered with a *Yes, sir,* the tight string inside of her snapped. She threw her head back, arching into his touch as she groaned his name toward the ceiling.

"Oh, thank God," he breathed, and then he was right on her heels. His free hand covered hers where she gripped him, stilling her movement and squeezing her fingers even more tightly around him as he ejaculated into her hand.

Her eyes flew to his face, and she watched his features completely relax, and he smiled beautifully at her with sparking eyes throughout his long, long orgasm.

When his body stilled, he leaned in and kissed her gently. He pulled back and landed her with another of those smiles.

Dahlia was finding it hard to breathe. She pulled her hand from his pants and wiggled until he pulled his own hand from hers. All of the things she'd been feeling right before the Impulse had taken over rushed back in, and Dahlia felt her own smile twist and turn sour.

Just a few moments ago, this man had informed her that he was dragging her away from her son. Today. Possibly right now. And she'd just done this . . . admittedly incredible thing with him. She pinned him with a glare.

His smile lost some of its wattage before dimming completely. She could tell the moment he returned to his senses, because a look of horror crossed his face. His mouth tightened into a grim line, and his eyebrows rose quickly, and then crashed down over his now flat, lifeless eyes. But before the coldness of his regard could completely destroy her, she saw a look of pure longing flash through his eyes. He clenched his fists and resumed straightening his clothing.

Shit. She watched as he did up his pants, his still semi-hard erection a visible bulge that made her swallow thickly despite the resentment nearly choking her. But what was almost worse was the confusion she saw in his eyes when just moments ago he had been looking at her as though she was the most radiant thing in his life.

She wanted the hate gone. Dahlia opened her mouth without thought. "The secret is at the Needles Research Facility," she said.

Chapter Nine

Dahlia's words pierced the litany of Jericho's self-loathing, and his hands froze where they had been zipping up his fly.

He refused to look at her—he was so confused over what he was feeling and thinking, over what they'd just done together—but he did manage to clear his throat around the thickness to ask, "The Research Facility?"

He felt her nod.

He closed his eyes as the confusion took over again. God, did he hate her? Love her? Believe her? Distrust her?

Right now, he realized with a groan, the answer appeared to be yes—to all of the above.

What had just happened had been the most amazing that had ever happened to him. Spilling into her hand, feeling her silky, slick skin beneath his fingers . . . had been life-changing.

The first coherent thought he'd had after climaxing so hard he'd nearly died there in the kitchen where they'd run the risk of being caught had been, *God, Emily would have never let me do this.*

And that had been when the horror had rushed in.

Comparing his Emily—his sweet, innocent Emily—with the human tornado of seduction that was Dahlia, even though it had been a subconscious comparison, had felt like knives to his gut.

And what was worse was he'd immediately thought *I'll regret what I've just done for the rest of my life* and known that thought was a complete lie. Oh, he'd remember this time in the kitchen with Dahlia forever, but he suspected regret would not be the emotion he associated with it.

He heard Dahlia's clothes rustle as she began putting herself back together, and Jericho forced himself to pay attention to what she'd just said, to what his entire purpose here was tied to.

He braced himself and flicked his eyes to her form, immediately taking in the obvious discomfort that painted her cheeks an embarrassed shade of red.

Well, at least their explosive reaction to each other hadn't shocked just him. She had yet to meet his eyes.

"I'm ready to tell you now," she said in a whisper, and it took Jericho a second to remember what they'd been discussing as something inside of him urged Jericho to put her at ease—an urge he immediately dismissed as absurd.

"I'm ready to listen," Jericho said as he leaned his hip against the counter and crossed his arms over his chest, affecting a pose he hoped said he was all business when he felt anything but.

Still without looking at him, Dahlia said, "Major Taylor hid something in the basement of the Needles facility."

Jericho straightened. He'd been expecting—hell, he wasn't sure what he'd been expecting her to share with him. Fluff. Something she'd made up to trick him.

Actual information that might help the Operation had been at the bottom of the list. He'd just gotten very interested.

"Okay," he said hoarsely, "you've got my attention. What did Taylor hide?"

Dahlia looked at him briefly, but her eyes skittered away from his face to stare blandly at a point over his shoulder. "I'm not sure, exactly," she began, "but, the way he talked about it, I think it was a weapon."

Jericho's gut dropped. Had Taylor planted a warhead in the middle of a civilian area? He wouldn't put it past the bastard.

His line of thoughts must have been obvious because Dahlia was quick to reassure him. "No, a weapon that was only dangerous to Eli," she clarified. She didn't pause before continuing. "Taylor was working under the assumption that it was the only thing that could kill an immortal."

Jericho felt his mouth drop.

"He was going to begin using it on Eli at the next experiment," she finished, her eyes flicking to his face and then back over his shoulder again.

Jericho forced his mouth closed again. *A weapon that could kill us?*

He immediately wanted to reject the idea; nothing could kill them. Eli's torture was proof of that. But, Jericho had always had a suspicion that the Trees would never have existed without some sort of balance—something to keep the world order.

His breath left him in a whoosh. "Wow," he said. "Okay, so we're going to the facility."

Dahlia nodded, but a look passed over her face that looked something close to nausea. In a heartbeat, Jericho knew Dahlia wanted to be nowhere near the location of her crimes.

His resolve strengthened. *Well, tough.* That feeling hadn't deterred her from her crimes, and it wouldn't deter Jericho from dragging her right back to the scene.

Relief that he was finally back on track with his orders crowded through him, pushing the confusion he had been feeling over the last few minutes into the back of his mind. "We leave in ten," he said brusquely to Dahlia, waiting for her nod of acknowledgement before heading into his room.

He closed the door quickly and dialed Eli's number for the second time that day, glad that this time he would actually have something to report. He studiously ignored the fact that he'd had something to report the first time as the phone rang in his ear.

Eli picked up immediately. "That was fast," his friend said, his tone obviously pleased.

Jericho relayed the information he'd gotten from Dahlia and let Eli know they were headed over to the facility right away.

"God," Eli said. "You've gotta be kidding me. That man's evil is *still* haunting me." Eli's shuddering breath echoed through the phone. "We need it—whatever it is—here at the base so we can secure it and figure out what exactly makes it tick. *And* to see if that crazy son of a bitch was right about what it does."

Jericho agreed. They finalized the plans—Eli assured Jericho the armed guard at the Needles Facility would be expecting them—and then Jericho remembered he had more intel to share.

"I have a new theory on how the Knowledge works," Jericho said hesitantly.

Eli got really quiet. Finally, "A new theory, huh?"

"Eli," Jericho began, then paused, not quite believing what he was about to say himself. "Last night, the Knowledge told me Dahlia was . . . *good*."

Silence. "But, she's not," Eli said.

"Now hear me out," Jericho said quickly. "Dahlia said something . . . it got me thinking. What if the Knowledge wasn't based on what a person *was*, but what they were currently doing? What their intentions were?"

Eli sighed heavily into the phone, and Jericho knew he'd lost him.

"Just think about it," Jericho said before Eli could shoot the theory down. "At the very least, it's something to test once I haul her back to base."

Eli's sigh this time was one of relief, and Jericho realized that the doubt that he would stick to orders was lurking in his friend's thoughts. That knowledge stung.

They ended their conversation, and Jericho walked out into the living room to find Dahlia waiting for him. "Let's go," he said shortly. "Give me the keys. I'll drive; you navigate."

Dahlia looked at him for several seconds, and he could tell in an instant that she'd shaken the embarrassment and uncertainty of earlier when she snapped, "Drive what, dip shit?"

Jericho frowned.

"We don't have a car," Dahlia said. "We use our money to eat."

Jericho's eyes roamed around the spartan living room, taking in the decay of the furnishings, the lack of decoration. Shame swarmed over him followed quickly by concern.

"You don't have a car?" he repeated woodenly. "But what if there's an emergency?"

Pure rage flashed across Dahlia's face, and Jericho realized he'd just insulted her ability to care for her family. She opened her mouth—probably to rip him a new one—but Jericho interrupted her. "Sorry," he said quickly. "Look, it doesn't matter. Quick fix."

Then he stormed out of the house with purpose, Dahlia close on his heels.

*

An hour later they were sitting in the office of the local Ford dealership as Jericho paid—with a *personal check*—for a brand new Super Duty truck totaling close to fifty grand. The man hadn't even batted an eyelash at the quoted price, had done an abysmal job of negotiating ("That seems fair"), and had pulled out a pen.

The amount of money he'd spent in a heartbeat made Dahlia ill. Just who in the hell was this guy? Even the dealer seemed dazed.

All throughout their dealings, Jericho kept brushing up against her—she could swear it was purposeful—and flashing his teeth at her in a mix between a grin and a grimace. It was slowly driving her crazy. Each contact was much too brief, and then she would get upset with herself for missing his touch. Her nerves were strung to their breaking point.

The final paperwork was done in a flash. Nothing got people to move quickly like someone throwing an obscene amount of money around.

Before she knew it, she was sitting in the passenger side of the truck and they were trundling through the desert right at the speed limit.

"You're quiet," he said in a grumbly, grouchy voice. They hadn't spoken to each other since leaving the house, and now Jericho was breaking the silence.

Dahlia had so much on her mind, but she didn't know a polite way of asking, "Why the fuck do you have that kind of money?"

When Jericho snapped his head back, she realized she'd said the words out loud. She sighed. Well, at least it saved her from having to find the polite way to ask the question. Manners had never been her thing.

"Oh, um—" Jericho stuttered. "Did that make you uncomfortable?" He was looking at her intently, his eyes a hybrid mixture of resentment and concern.

The man was actually worried that he'd made Dahlia uncomfortable by spending a lot of money.

She laughed unkindly. "Yeah, you could say that." Considering the only people she knew with that kind of money broke the law. A lot.

"That's not what I intended. I'm sorry. I just wanted the safest possible car for you and Gabriel, and having the truck will make life that much easier."

Dahlia couldn't believe her ears. "I'm sorry—for *me and Gabriel?*" she could hear her voice was loud as it rang throughout the cab.

Jericho frowned and . . . blushed? "Well, yeah. You guys needed a car."

Dahlia looked out the car windshield and tried to breathe slowly and steadily. It didn't work. "No. Stop the car. Turn around. We're taking it back." She waited for him to immediately follow her direction. After a full minute when the truck had not slowed down at all, she finally forced herself to face him again.

When he saw she was looking at him, he said simply, "No."

"*No?* You think this is a negotiation? I don't want or need your help, and I do not accept *cars* from people who drag me away from my son. So turn the fucking car around or so help me I will—punch your . . . leg."

Well, that had sounded sufficiently less bad-ass than she'd planned.

However, it appeared to have worked because he pulled the truck over to the shoulder. He didn't even look at her. That muscle in his jaw was throbbing again. "Dahlia," he began, "you're not going to win this argument, okay? I know you're mad and upset at how this is going to end up, but this is the least I can do. It's not a handout—it's reparation. And if you need to punch my leg all the way to and from the facility, well, I think I can handle that."

Then he nodded his head as though he was just now agreeing with what he'd said, turned to the road again, and pulled them back onto the interstate.

Oh, he was in so much trouble. Buying a truck in no way made up for dragging her away from Gabriel. But she was more upset that she'd lost an argument. She couldn't remember the last time she'd lost an argument. And who the hell wins an argument by literally saying to the opponent *you're not going to win this argument?* That seemed . . . underhanded.

She fumed silently as they drove across the desert, plotting ways to make him eat his damn truck.

They arrived at the facility far too quickly for her tastes. She'd been so distracted by her thoughts that she hadn't had time to mentally prepare for being back here. Every muscle in her body clenched at the sight of the building.

She did not want to be here. Had promised herself that she would never have to come back. And here she was.

It was all worth it to save Gabriel.

The two posted military guards allowed them to pass through the high-security checkpoint, and then much too soon, they were walking toward one of the most evil places Dahlia had ever encountered.

Dahlia had instinctively moved closer to Jericho as he walked through the doors of the run-down old building. She mentally chastised herself and forced herself to maintain a normal amount of distance. Jericho noticed her movement and glanced at her curiously while he walked leisurely through the hall, gazing into rooms, and moving on quickly.

Dahlia thought she might vomit. They were getting close.

They made it through the entire civilian portion of the building before Jericho turned to her and asked, "Where to?"

This was the part where she lost Jericho forever. Pain coursed through her before she drew herself up short. *Lost him forever?* She didn't want him. For any amount of time. Another pang of pain followed that thought.

She shook herself. She had to get this over with and get out of here. The walls felt like they were closing in, their evil a tangible thing. Dahlia braced herself and turned to walk to the supply closet. "Follow me," she said, not looking behind her to make sure he did.

She walked into the dark room. All of the medical supplies had fallen from the shelves to lie in a pile on the floor. And against the far wall, the shelving hung haphazardly from the corner of the room revealing a staircase that descended into the dark.

The light switch didn't work when she tried it. Jericho looked at her askance and silently pulled the flashlight from his belt, clicking it on and pointing it down the stairs.

Dahlia did the same. *Here goes nothing.* She followed him into the abyss.

The safety glass that separated the lab from the staircase threw the beams of their flashlights back at them. They quickly moved through the open door and entered the main lab. Their twin beams arced over the ground, hitting what looked to be props from a horror movie. The ground and walls were littered with bone saws, a toppled stretcher with leather restraints, x-ray films, surgical implements, and the overwhelming essence of pain and fear.

Jericho cursed long and low. And then the moment she'd been dreading arrived: through the dim, yellow light of the flashlights, Dahlia watched his eyes make their way slowly through the refuse on the ground to find her, and he looked at her with horror.

"What happened here?" he asked hoarsely.

Dahlia closed her eyes briefly. When she opened them again, she was surprised to find that Jericho's shadowy form was blurry.

"Terrible things," she whispered.

He stepped toward her, his boots crunching on the glass, until he stood right before her. His eyes were glittery and bright. "Terrible things for Eli or for you?"

The question caught her completely off guard. She reeled back in shock, and something inside of her fought back against his unexpected kindness. "*For me?*" she asked hysterically. "I *am* this, Jericho. I helped Major Taylor do this to Eli! *I'm* the bad guy, not the victim."

His eyes searched hers for several minutes, and his arm rose leadenly toward her, his fingers brushed her cheek, and just as the Knowledge whispered *good* to her, Jericho's face flashed relief. And Dahlia realized why he had been brushing against her so much in the last few hours. He was trying to identify her. The only thing that surprised her in this was that he was obviously pleased with his findings—and that could only mean that the Knowledge had been telling Jericho that she was good.

She frowned. But she wasn't. No one knew that better than her.

Jericho's finger brushed past her cheek and ear and into her hair. She couldn't resist leaning into his hand and she tried to anchor herself against her roiling emotions. What the hell was going on?

"It's over now, Dahlia," he whispered to her.

She jerked her head away before the Impulse made her do something stupid. What had happened in this room would never be over. Not for her. She focused on a point over Jericho's shoulder when his eyes grew to be too much for her. "It's buried in the wall," she said roughly.

Jericho sighed, a sad sound, and dropped his hand.

*

Oh, this woman was tying him into knots. Even now, watching the self-loathing cross her face every few minutes, Jericho was caught between passionate hate for her and passionate . . . passion. The small taste of her he'd gotten in the kitchen had deeply affected him. He didn't know up from down. And damned if he hated seeing her in this lab. His instinct fought with him, making him long to protect her from this horrible place.

He cast his eyes around the walls, seeing no indication of what she'd just said. "In the wall?" he repeated.

She nodded and then walked over to the wall. "Hidden right in here," she said as she laid her hand against the rough cement wall.

The wall beneath her hand suddenly began to flicker with light. An unease settled into Jericho's stomach, and he sprinted over to her and snatched her hand from the wall.

The flickering continued. They both stared at the wall.

"It's never done . . . *that* . . . before," she whispered uneasily.

Their eyes met and held for a few seconds. "Stand back," Jericho whispered. She moved back several feet and shined her flashlight on the wall. Jericho located an axe—the use of an axe in Eli's imprisonment caused momentary unease—and he approached the wall with purpose.

Jericho heaved the axe over his shoulder and put all of his strength into the first swing. The wall completely crumbled under the axe. Jericho stumbled back from the exertion he hadn't needed. "Fast-drying cement," he said to himself.

A gaping hole hovered in the wall about chest-height. The flickering they'd seen against the back of the cement was now full color and filling the lab with light.

Dahlia edged closer to the wall and tried to look into the hole, but Jericho snatched her back.

She glared at him, and Jericho half-smiled sheepishly. "Sorry. Let me look first, okay?"

Dahlia rolled her eyes, but she nodded and let him lean in to look.

After several seconds of silence, she finally snapped, "Well, what is it?"

"Um . . . " he tore his eyes away to look back at her briefly before gazing through the hole again. "It's . . . a sword."

Jericho gawked at it in a trance. Green and gold flames traveled up and down the blade of the sword, casting wavering light around the inside of the hole. With the utmost caution, he snaked a hand through the jagged concrete and gripped the handle. Jericho knew everything there was to know about guns, but not swords. However, even he could tell that this weapon was old. Way older than either of them; way older than anything he'd ever seen.

Holy fuck. What had Major Taylor been up to?

"What *is* it?" Dahlia asked.

"I think it's a broadsword." Jericho's said.

Okay, so Major Taylor had hidden a flaming broadsword in the basement of his evil lair. That did not bode well.

Jericho leaned forward and squinted his eyes. "There's writing on the blade," he said. He ran his fingertips along the broad edge of the blade. "I can't read it. The writing's in a different language." And then he snatched his hand back with a hiss as pain flared.

Dahlia shone her beam on Jericho's hand and gasped as she took two stumbling steps toward him. He halted her with a quick, "Stay back!"

She stopped.

"It's just a little knick," he said, trying to assure her with a smile. "It's sharp, and I was careless, that's all."

She obviously didn't believe him. Jericho leaned over at the waist and placed the sword gently on the ground, and then he backed away from it. "We're going to leave this right here, okay? I don't want you anywhere near it."

He grabbed her hand, the Knowledge that she was *good* quickly flaring, and tugged her toward the staircase where she finally tore her eyes away from the sword to watch where she was going.

"We can't just leave it here," she protested.

"Absolutely right," he said. "I'm calling it in. Eli needs to know about this. Someone way more qualified than me needs to come in and collect that with the proper equipment."

She snorted. "Proper equipment for *that*?"

They'd reached the top of the stairs, but Jericho didn't slow down as he pulled her through the remainder of the facility.

When they reached the outside, Jericho kept walking, pulling her right to the truck, where he opened the passenger door and handed her in. He felt the oppression of the building slip from his shoulders in the open air, and watched as Dahlia rolled her own shoulders and breathed a sigh of relief.

"Sorry, I just had to get you out of there," he mumbled. "I didn't want you anywhere close to that thing. It was bad enough looking at you standing in the middle of that room."

Dahlia closed her eyes, her expression betraying a sense of defeat, but Jericho didn't pause to ponder it. He pulled his cellphone from his back pocket and dialed Eli's number. "It's me," he said into the phone. "The weapon is a flaming sword," he said, still in shocked disbelief.

Eli took over with a barrage of questions that Jericho answered without thought. They arranged for pick-up in full hazmat suits.

The conversation wound down and then there was dead silence on the phone for several seconds. Finally, Eli asked, "Okay, so is there anything else? Anything to keep you from bringing her back right away?"

Time stood still. Jericho's eyes flew to Dahlia's again, and—just his luck—she was staring straight at him.

Jericho paused, a feeling of heavy responsibility falling on him. His eyes flicked away from Dahlia. "No, I haven't found out anything else. But I think I could. I'd like permission to pursue further intel."

From his peripheral vision, he saw Dahlia snap to attention, but he couldn't focus on what she was overhearing. The sickness that swept in with his lies nearly debilitated him.

Eli said nothing for several more seconds. "I can't promise anything," Eli said slowly.

Jericho would take what he could get. "Okay, thanks," he said as he hung up.

He braced himself and then looked at Dahlia, silently begging her to say nothing with his eyes.

"You lied for me," she said in a whisper.

Jericho nodded.

"Why?" she asked.

He looked at her for several seconds, and then he shifted his eyes to the ground, studying his boots. "I don't know," he said in a small voice.

He continued to look at the ground, studiously avoiding her gaze. But then, her hand moved through the space that divided them from each other. He watched as her hand splayed on his chest.

His head shot up, instant heat flaring through his body, the Impulse kicking to full life.

Dahlia licked her lips, fisted her hand in his shirt, and dragged him to her.

Chapter Ten

Before he could realize what was happening, her lips were crushed against his, and she was licking at their seam.

He opened his lips automatically, without thought, and was immediately rewarded when her tongue slipped inside his mouth and swept hungrily across the roof of his mouth.

He groaned at the sensation. All of the stress of the last few hours released him from its grip, and his arms flew up and surrounded her. He jerked her to him with no finesse, sliding her across the truck's seat, needing to feel her flush against him, needing to forget what he'd just done. One hand splayed in the small of her back, the other hand rose up through the cool waves of her hair to grab a handful and wrap it around his wrist.

He tugged gently, pulling her head further back, and he knew her neck would be arched beautifully. He pulled back from the kiss to glance at it, and then he lowered his head again to nibble down her neck from ear to collarbone.

She squirmed against him and tried to lean back on the truck bench and pull him back with her, and for some reason, this movement was enough to bring him back to where they were. Maybe it was the desire he had to crawl atop her, part her legs, and drive himself home that made him remember that they were out in public.

With more strength than he thought he had, he pulled from Dahlia's kiss, forced his hand to release her hair, and glanced up and over the dashboard to find two very amused guards watching them from the gate.

"What?" Dahlia asked from her propped up position on the seat. "Why're we stopping?"

Jericho returned his attention to her again, and smiled at what he saw. Her lips were kiss-swollen, her hair was mussed from his hand, and somehow he'd managed to raise her shirt over her bra without realizing it.

She looked delectable, confused, and frustrated.

"We have an audience," he said and nodded his head toward the guards.

Her expression didn't change, and he realized she wasn't thinking clearly enough to care. He leaned down and gave her one brief kiss— anything more would try his control—and pulled her shirt down. "Scooch up," he told her gently. When she didn't move at all, he chuckled and helped her sit up and turn around. He shut her door and jogged around the hood to his side of the truck, the movements of his body causing a rather insistent body part to rub painfully. He pointedly ignored the guards and slid into the driver's seat.

As soon as the door was closed, Dahlia scooted over to him, her hand falling directly to the crotch of his pants where she closed her hand over his length.

He hissed in a breath through his clenched teeth. He had to get them somewhere private. Now. He started the car with a violent crank of the key and reversed so quickly he spit up chunks of asphalt.

He left the facility like a man possessed while Dahlia leaned in further and bit down on his neck, sucking hard. Her hand moved up and down his length rigorously, and Jericho thought briefly that there was a very real possibility he was going to crash the car. He made it about half a mile down the road before finding an abandoned neighborhood to pull off into.

The car was barely in park before Jericho lost control. Dahlia let out a quick squeak as Jericho turned on her, launching them back into the bench and cramming his hips between her legs.

"God, Dahlia," he knew he was being too rough, just like the last time. It had never been this way with Emily. He couldn't figure out why he had no control over his actions, why he mauled Dahlia whenever he got the opportunity.

But, thank God, she didn't seem to mind. She gave him an answering moan and wrapped her arms around his shoulders and sifted her fingers through his hair. "You're back," she whispered against his lips. "Thank God."

Yep, she liked it. The quarters were cramped, but Jericho didn't care. His boots hit against the driver's side window with percussive thumps, and already their heavy breathing was fogging up the interior of the car, making the air thick.

He'd never done anything like this in a car before, and he vowed right there and then to do it repeatedly in the future. But only with Dahlia.

She was nibbling on his lower lip, her hands traveling from his hair to trail over his shoulders, down his biceps, skittering over to his lower back and then down to his ass, where she grabbed him hard, her finger tips digging into the flesh through his pants.

His hips kicked forward, thrusting into the heated center between her legs. She moaned and arched her back. "God, yes," she muttered, biting down on his lip harder.

A harsh noise sounded from the back of his throat, and his thrust again. And again. He was spiraling out of control, and he quickly realized he had about one and half more thrusts before orgasm.

He pulled his lip from her teeth and looked at her anxiously. She needed more than he could give her if he didn't quit moving. He groaned and pulled his erection from its favorite place. He needed an idea. God, he hated not knowing what he was doing. She was obviously experienced, and he wasn't good enough for her.

She moaned in protest when he moved from her, licking and biting her lips. His eyes zeroed in to her mouth, and the idea suddenly hit him. The idea was so tempting, he almost didn't need the extra thrust and a half to finish, and he gritted his teeth and prayed for control.

He scooted back further, and fit his arms beneath her body,

lifting her gently to prop her up against the passenger side door.

Then, with shaky fingers, he reached for the button of her pants. She saw the direction he was headed, groaned in excitement and added her fingers to the task. Four hands fumbled with her fly until her pants were open.

She lifted her ass quickly, and Jericho grabbed her pants and began sliding them down her hips. When her pants moved to reveal red lacy panties that he'd only felt this morning, Jericho cursed and all semblance of gentleness evaporated.

His vision tunneled. He distantly heard the fabric of her pants rip, and—thank fuck—her pants were off. He dove to the bench, landing on his belly and chest between her legs and face-planting on those delicious, lacy panties.

Dahlia cried out above him, her hands flew to his hair and grabbed two handfuls roughly. The pain from her grip felt wonderful. He buried his face further between her legs and inhaled slowly, her arousal the best perfume he'd ever smelled. He pressed fevered kisses to the fabric covering her cleft, and she squirmed beneath his touch.

His hands flew to her hips and gripped tightly as he held her still so he could swipe his tongue from bottom to top over the lace. She bucked in his grip.

"Jericho, please," she begged him.

He licked her panties again to let her know he'd heard her, and then he moved his fingers down from her hips to the waistband of her underwear. He continued to press kisses to the crotch of her panties as he slowly rolled her underwear down until his mouth halted its progress. He drew back to pull the panties the rest of the way off. Dahlia bent her legs to accommodate him in the small space, and soon, the skimpy red lace was dangling off his index finger.

He looked at her, the panties between them. She was panting against the door. A few locks of her wavy hair had traveled over her shoulders and in front of her face, and her breaths puffed them out in rapid succession. Her eyes were glazed over with passion and hooded.

He made sure she watched as he slowly brought her panties to his face. He pressed them over his nose and mouth and inhaled, his eyes closing slowly at the pleasure of her scent.

He heard her suck in a breath, felt her legs jolt on either side of his knees. He opened his eyes again and looked at her solemnly as he placed the panties in his pants' pocket. He hoped they weren't her favorites, because she was *never* getting them back. That business handled, he finally allowed his eyes to look at her exposed sex.

She was sprawled before him. Her knees were slightly bent and wide open, one resting on the dashboard, the other wedged between his hips and the seat back. Her lips were spread and glistening. She was completely hairless.

Jericho felt his mouth drop, and he groaned from deep in his chest. "Holy God, Dahlia," he whispered, his fingers traveling with a mind of their own to brush over the hill of her mound reverently.

She shuddered with his unpracticed touch, and Jericho felt a burst of pride that even though he was completely clueless, he seemed to be pleasing her. Greatly. She grabbed his hand frantically and pressed it more fully against the very top of her cleft, right over the achingly swollen bud he could plainly see throbbing.

He jerked his hand away quickly before he could lose his purpose. Her skin was smooth, slick. If he touched her for one second longer, he would forget what he planned to do. And he *really* didn't want to forget.

He smiled at her slowly and shook his head. He was nervous as hell, but he didn't want her to know, so he simply said, "Not what I had in mind, sweetheart."

And then he fell to his belly again, putting his face right where it had just been, only now, there was no barrier between his lips and her core—just the way he wanted it.

He knew the moment he kissed her, he was a goner—would have no finesse, would simply devour her—so he vowed to take it as slowly as he could here at the beginning.

Her hands were already in his hair again, tugging him forward. He lazily brought one of his wide palms to hers, enclosing both of her wrists in one hand, and pulling them gently to his lips, he kissed her finger tips and then directed one hand to grip the back of the seat, the other to the dashboard. "Patience," he whispered.

She breathed a disbelieving laugh, and he realized that she thought he was talking to her. That was fine. Let her think he was in control. This close to her center, her scent was overwhelming him, and he wasn't sure he could hold out much longer. He was terrified that he'd be overcome and plow into her with his aching erection instead of just pleasuring her with his mouth as he'd planned.

Her hands secured, he returned his attention to the prize before his face. The sun streaming through the windshield cast her skin in a display of diamonds, picking up on the caramel highlights and lowlights.

"You're exquisite," he breathed. She shifted uncomfortably, apparently anxious about his perusal, and he wondered who the hell she had been with in the past that no one had worshiped her like this. He knew he was going to do it frequently and for the rest of their lives.

The thought penetrated the lust-fog of his mind, and he nearly choked as he gasped. He was already thinking of the rest of his life with this woman? He frowned as he tried to think back to the past, to the first time he'd experienced the Impulse eight years ago.

He remembered in shock that he'd fallen deeply in love with Emily the moment he'd laid eyes on her and heard the Voice whisper "the One" to him. In comparison, falling for Dahlia was taking an eon.

Holy shit. He was falling for Dahlia! Despite her possibly evil nature, her secrets, her less-than-sweet personality.

And that was all the thinking he accomplished before the lust came roaring back in, with even more force now that he'd discovered he had strong feelings for the woman spread before him like a banquet.

He grinned and then blew a gentle stream of air over her, starting just below her belly button and then traveling down slowly until just reaching the top of her cleft. She wiggled again and moaned, so he resumed his stream of air, this time passing down her parted flesh and back up.

She cried out, and he heard her nails scrape across the dashboard and the leather of the seat back creak.

He closed the small distance between them and pressed a chaste kiss to the very top of her, right over that bud.

"Jericho," she moaned. "Please, don't tease me. I can't take it anymore."

He hadn't realized he'd been teasing; he'd just been taking his time, enjoying her. But he couldn't ignore her pleas, would give her anything she wanted, and so her returned to kiss her again. This time, nervously, with an open mouth over her bud and a swift swipe of his tongue.

He dimly heard her cry out so loudly it approached a scream, but his own guttural grunt overshadowed the noise she made.

Her taste. He'd never encountered anything so perfect. So made exactly for him. He kissed her again, and again. His hands returned to her hips, digging in hard. He grew frantic, his kisses more rapid.

"Lick me," she begged him.

He opened his mouth wide and lolly popped her from bottom to top. This time, there was no doubt that her cries had turned to screams.

"Jericho, *please*," she whimpered. "I need—"

It didn't matter that she couldn't finish her sentence. Jericho knew exactly what she needed. He licked her broadly one more time before focusing on her clit, lapping it in short strokes again and again. He heard himself moaning with every taste, louder and louder, and realized he was thrusting into the bench seat in time with his mouth. He was going to come, quickly, and harder than he ever had in his life.

He began thrusting harder, surging toward that finish that he needed more than he needed air. He simply *had* to finish at the same time that she did, and he could tell by her cries that she was close. She was repeating his name over and over in a prayerful litany.

Her hands returned to his hair, nails scraping across his scalp. He felt every muscle in her body tense, her breaths grow even shorter, her cries rise in pitch, and then she shattered beneath his tongue.

She arched from the door, grabbed his head and held him against her firmly while she undulated beneath his mouth. He sucked her nub between her lips and kissed her through the final waves of her orgasm, and he went over the edge too.

He shouted against her moist skin, stiffening and thrusting one final time. "Dahlia," he groaned. "God, oh, Dahlia." He muttered a stream of words he was unaware of, certain he was revealing feelings that he had not spoken of prior to this moment as he came and came and came.

Dahlia's violent grip on his head turned to caressing just as the ability for complex thought returned to Jericho. She brushed her fingers through his hair and sighed.

He raised his head, turned into her palm and kissed her before forcing himself upright on wobbly arms. He let out a shaky breath as he held out his right arm and beckoned her to him. She wrestled her pants back up—Jericho barely stopped a groan of complaint as she covered herself—and moved immediately though slowly into the curve of his body, wrapping her arms around him from the side and resting her head on his heaving chest. His arm curled around her and pulled her even closer, and he buried his nose in her hair while he tried to catch his breath.

"That was—" Dahlia began and then stopped.

Jericho closed his eyes and gritted his teeth, waiting for her verdict.

"The best thing I've ever experienced," she said so softly he almost didn't hear her. He could swear she sounded shocked and a little unsteady, and not just from the physical portion of what had just happened.

Jericho breathed a sigh of relief and gave her a reassuring squeeze. "For me, too," he whispered into her hair. And it had been. To his shame, he again made an immediate comparison to what his short encounter with Emily had been like. Both women had blown his mind, but Emily was sweet, fragile, and if Jericho was honest, not very passionate. The few days they'd been together, Jericho had felt the need to handle her like spun glass. And, unlike with Dahlia, he had been able to control himself enough with Emily to actually handle her gently. With Dahlia, he lost all control. "I didn't hurt you did I?" he asked quickly. God, he couldn't even remember how rough he'd been.

She pulled away and looked at him frankly. "Are you kidding me? No! And if you get any less enthusiastic, I'll kick your ass." And then she promptly snuggled back into his chest.

They held each other for several minutes. He eventually heard Dahlia begin to breathe evenly and realized she had fallen asleep.

He smiled and kissed her hair again, and keeping her just where she was, turned on the car and pointed them toward home.

*

Dahlia was warm, cozy, and more relaxed than she could remember being in nearly a decade. But she was being nudged persistently by someone who was going to die.

She groaned in warning and snuggled closer to the warmth next to her. The warmth chuckled, and Dahlia snapped to wakefulness.

Before her now-wide-open eyes was the t-shirt-clad chest of the man who had just shown her how things should be between a man and a woman. Holy shit, had that been incredible. She'd been with a lot of men in her quest to feel a connection, enough that next to the practically virginal

Jericho she felt ashamed, and also regretful, but she had never known anything like that.

She smiled slowly into Jericho's chest, breathed in his masculine scent and cuddled in closer.

"Sweetheart, we're home," Jericho said in a strained voice while his arm tightened about her and drew her closer. His lips fell to her hair fervently, and he kissed her once, twice, a third time before Dahlia raised her head and met his descending lips with her own. She sighed against him and he took the opportunity to slide his tongue into her mouth. She groaned, her arms moving to come around him—

"They're home, they're home," Gabriel shouted excitedly from somewhere outside the truck.

Dahlia jerked back, but Jericho was more relaxed, pressing one final kiss to her forehead and preventing her from pulling away from him completely. He smiled at her softly, and then he turned from her to open the car door, revealing a jumping-bean version of her son.

Gabriel bounced from foot to foot while Jericho climbed down. As soon as Jericho moved aside, Gabriel launched himself into the truck and at her.

All of the air oof-ed out of her, and then she returned her son's hug, looking at Jericho over Gabriel's mop of brown hair. He watched them through wary, squinty eyes before smiling reluctantly. She found herself smiling back, and for a second— just a second—she allowed herself to fantasize that they were a family. Gabriel was their son; this was their home; they belonged to each other.

It was such a powerful image it brought tears to her eyes. She tightened her hug involuntarily, and Gabriel squirmed.

"*Mamá*!" he protested. "Too tight!"

She loosened her arms. "Sorry, *mijo*."

"Where'd you get a *truck*?" he asked excitedly, bouncing up and down on her lap.

Before she could open her mouth, Jericho opened his. "It's *your* truck," he said. Gabriel's head swiveled around to him like a little owl. "What do you think?" Jericho asked.

Dahlia shot him a warning glare, but he pointedly ignored it, all of his attention focused on Gabriel.

"Really?" Gabriel squealed. "Can I drive it?"

Jericho quickly hid a smile and looked at her with an open face and shrugged. Gabriel turned toward her too, wearing an almost identical expression.

Oh, good God, they couldn't be serious. "No!" she shouted. "Are you both crazy?"

"Ah, *ma*—" Gabriel started in that whiney voice kids get when they want something outrageous.

"She said no, buddy," Jericho said, keeping his tone light. "Come on and help me carry some supplies into the backyard. I need your muscles."

And, like he hadn't been perched on the edge of an epic tantrum, Gabriel bounced out of the truck and followed Jericho to its bed emitting happy chatter.

Dahlia blinked. She was geared up, ready for some heavy parenting, and in four small words, Jericho had handled the situation for her. She closed her eyes. Oh, how badly she wanted the family fantasy. She had been without help all this time. In two short days, she feared she'd grown too dependent on Jericho's help.

She turned her head and saw that Jericho was lifting construction beams from the loaded bed of the truck. Gabriel was carrying a bag of small supplies. She frowned. Just how soundly had she slept? She didn't remember stopping for supplies. And why the hell did they even have supplies?

Jericho saw her watching them through the rear window and flashed a crooked grin that caused butterflies to dance in her stomach. He tossed three beams over his shoulder, balanced them with a gloved hand and then walked around the truck, Gabriel on his heels. "Come on, sleepyhead," he called to her as he passed.

Dahlia stumbled from the truck and went around to the bed to stare in bemusement at the overflow of construction supplies and equipment. She could only manage one beam.

She turned dumbly and followed Jericho and her son into the back yard. "What's all this stuff for?" she asked, recognizing the warning in her question. She knew something was up.

He winked at her. "I placed a call and arranged for pickup while you slept. I'll be able to fix the roof before nightfall."

She widened her eyes. A fixed roof?

"There are some groceries in the cab behind the seat," he continued. "Why don't you grab some and take them into the kitchen?"

Dahlia's stomach rumbled in response, and she realized she hadn't had lunch in all the . . . excitement of the day. Jericho smiled at her. "There's some ready-made stuff, too, so you can eat something now."

Without another word, Dahlia turned on her heel and walked back to the truck, her thoughts in turmoil.

Her jaw dropped as she peered behind the seat. He'd gotten enough groceries to feed three families.

She needed air. Now. Right now.

She stumbled into the house, knowing if she killed Jericho in front of her son she would cause psychological damage. Esperanza heard her and called to her from the kitchen. Dahlia walked in, ready to let loose to the woman Dahlia knew would understand her feelings.

She skidded to a stop. The kitchen gleamed, and there was a new gas-range stove and stainless steel refrigerator.

She stopped in her tracks. "*¿Que es todo esto?*" she said, asking Esperanza what those were.

"*Nuestro nuevo refrigerador y la estufa,*" Esperanza said, rubbing her hands together with childlike glee.

Well, yes, Dahlia could see that they were a refrigerator and stove. The real question was, what the hell were they doing in her kitchen?

Jericho came into the kitchen at that moment, carrying all of the groceries in his arms, a loaded tool belt slung low around his hips. "Oh, good," he said. "They came."

Dahlia spun around, suddenly way more angry than she remembered being in her life. With forced calm, she said, "Can I speak with you in the hall?"

Jericho's eyes immediately clouded with guardedness, but he nodded, placed the rest of the groceries on the counter where Esperanza was already working putting them away in the commercial-grade fridge.

As soon as they had the relative privacy of the hallway, Dahlia blew up. "Just what the hell do you think you're doing?"

Jericho sighed wearily, and not in surprise, which meant he knew she wouldn't be happy with the extravagant gift . . . and he'd done it anyway. Her anger reached new levels.

"Look, Dahlia, I can't stand the thought of you and Gabriel living in this house the way it is."

Shame at the condition she was living in—that *Gabriel* was having to live in—flooded her. "Well, *Jericho*," she spat his name at him, immediately going on the offense, "you don't get a vote. You're taking me away soon, and then you'll never see us again, so just send it all back and *stop doing this shit*!" The final words had escalated to a screech, and Dahlia tried to force herself to calm down.

Jericho rubbed his chest in slow circles, a frown on his face. "I know what I'm going to do. Do you have to keep bringing it up?" he muttered, and Dahlia couldn't help thinking he didn't know he was speaking aloud.

"*Mamá*," Gabriel shouted as he rounded the curve into the hallway at a dead run. "Did you see our new stuff?"

Dahlia closed her eyes and tried to focus on her breathing so she wouldn't attack Jericho in front of her child. When she opened them again, it was to see Gabriel and Jericho were both looking at her, something akin to hero-worship for Jericho reflected in Gabriel's eyes. It was enough to make her sick. Jericho's expression clearly read, *What are you going to do now*? Gabriel's expression was just confused, obviously not understanding why

Dahlia wasn't as excited as he and Esperanza were.

She gritted her teeth. Jericho had manufactured this, damn him. He knew she wouldn't snatch these things out of the hands of her son once he'd seen them. He was manipulating the situation, and she didn't care for it at all.

"*Mijo, ve y ayunda a tu abuela.*" As Gabriel jogged off to help Esperanza finish unpacking groceries, Dahlia walked up to Jericho until they were nose-to-nose.

"I really hate it when I can't understand you guys," he said, almost to himself. "I need to learn Spanish."

Dahlia smacked him in the chest. "Don't bother, you'll be out of our lives in a matter of days. And thank *God* I'll never have to see you again." She was fuming. "Listen to me, and listen to me good, you stubborn, manipulating *cabrón*. You get one more thing for this house and then use my son to force me into accepting it, and I'll throw you out on your *culo*, you got me? And I'll make sure you never find us again!"

Jericho's face fell. "You think I'm *manipulating* you?" he asked in a horrified whisper.

"That's exactly what you're doing, and don't pretend otherwise."

"No, Dahlia. Just . . . *no*! That wasn't my intention at all. I just have all this damn money from the government for what happened to me and—" He stopped.

His mate.

"It's dirty money, and I don't want it. It made me feel better to spend it on you . . . and Gabriel." He was looking at the floor now, but she could see he was still frowning.

Dahlia was speechless. Was he telling the truth, or was this just another part of his male manipulation? She honestly didn't know, and it frightened her. It had been ages since she'd been able to be fooled by a man, and the thought that some of her savviness might have vanished frightened her to no end. How was she going to survive if she had gone back to her pre-Gabriel days?

She had to know, so she stretched out her hand and brushed it down his arm lightly. His head snapped up, and he tried to reach for her, but she jerked back. She'd gotten what she needed. The Knowledge had told her Jericho was *good*. Still. Probably always.

Oh, shit, she was in deep. She had no idea how to handle a good man. She envisioned arguments like the one they'd just had occurring over and over again for the rest of their lives until she finally drove him away with her distrust—

And then she remembered that he was going to be going away anyway. In a couple of days when he took her back to the compound. She knew she would never be able to forgive him for taking her away from Gabriel. And so things would end then. No matter what.

"Don't do it again," she whispered. "I can take care of my son."

Jericho's eyes still looked bleak, but he nodded despite obviously wanting to argue.

"And speaking of my son," Dahlia charged on, her voice rising once again as she remembered how Gabriel had looked at Jericho. "If you get him to love you, to depend on you, and then you hurt him, I will castrate you with my bare hands, *comprende*?"

Jericho's nostrils flared, and she saw undefinable emotion in his eyes. "Of course," he said in a gravelly voice. "You're right."

Without another word, he turned on his heel and walked into the kitchen.

Dahlia watched him go. Against her will and her temper, her eyes ate up the wide expanse of his back, the narrowing of his hips, the way his ass moved beneath the seat of his pants, and she sighed. Why did she feel like the bad guy in this?

Chapter Eleven

Later that night, Jericho sprawled on his back in the floor of the empty guest room and propped his head up with one arm behind his neck.

Twenty-four hours ago, he had been someone entirely different than he was today: a soldier who knew his job and would never shirk from completing it.

But now? He shook himself mentally. *No.* He was still a soldier, he still knew his job, and he would *not* shirk from completing it.

The worst thing that had happened today was Dahlia warning him off her son.

His gut clenched. Jericho blew out a frustrated breath. So he had to cut off interaction with the kid. So what? No one said he had to like it, he just had to do it. He threw himself onto his side and focused on steadying his breathing so he could drop off into some much-needed sleep.

Sleep was long in coming, but when it did finally come, it was quickly interrupted. Jericho was jerked to consciousness by the brush of something on his arm.

Years of training kept him still until he had determined the threat. It took only three seconds for him to realize Gabriel had woken him up.

"Hey, buddy," Jericho said.

"I had a bad dream." Gabriel's voice was shaky and small.

Jericho closed his eyes again. *Distance.* He had to keep the kid at a distance.

Gabriel's broken breathing had Jericho opening his eyes again and pulling himself into a seated position. "A bad dream?"

Jericho could see Gabriel's silhouette nod.

Shit. What did Gabriel need from him? What was he supposed to do? "Do you want to tell me about it?" Jericho asked hesitantly.

Gabriel shook his head, but the words tumbled from his mouth anyway. "Mommy was gone, and you weren't there to save me."

"Save you?" Jericho frowned. *From what?* "Well, Mommy is here, and so am I. You're safe. I promise."

But the air dripped with Gabriel's doubt. Jericho sighed and scooted back until his back hit the wall. "Here," Jericho patted his knee. "I'll sit up with you until you fall asleep again, okay?"

It was obviously the purpose behind Gabriel's visit, because the kid scrambled over and practically threw himself into Jericho's lap. Jericho reached beyond him and grabbed the blanket, making sure the boy was covered. Then he leaned his head against the wall and waited for Gabriel to fall asleep so he could take him back to his own room.

So much for distance.

*

Gabriel was gone.

Dahlia clamped a hand over her mouth to keep the scream inside as she stared down at her son's rumpled, empty bed. Oh, God, it had happened. He'd found them.

Her first coherent thought was to get Jericho. Jericho would help her. Her second thought was *hell, no*, but she was so desperate that she willingly threw aside her need for independence in favor of her son's safety.

She tore down the hallway to Jericho's room. The door was open, so she didn't have to slow down. She grabbed the doorframe and swung into the room at full speed . . .

Only to screech to a halt.

Across the room against the far wall, Jericho was sleeping sitting up. His head was tilted back at what looked to be an incredibly painful angle. His mouth was wide open, and his snores rent the morning air.

Curled up with his head on Jericho's knee was her son.

Dahlia was so shocked and relieved to find him in Jericho's room that she didn't immediately react. She was able to take in Gabriel's peaceful sleeping face. Jericho's hand on the boy's head. They looked . . . like they belonged together. Like a family.

Dahlia lost her shit.

She stomped over to Jericho and poked him in the shoulder. "*Tss*," she hissed at him through her teeth.

She knew he had woken up, because he stiffened. But he didn't move. After several long seconds, he opened his eyes slowly, as though he didn't have a care in the world. His sleepy eyes caused her gut to clench.

Which only made her more furious. "What the *fuck* is my son doing in here?" she whisper-yelled at him.

That woke him up. He raised his head with a jerk and looked at Gabriel's sleeping form. He cursed softly.

Dahlia nodded. "That's right, sunshine. Feeling the life of a eunuch, hmm?"

Gabriel slept on blissfully as Jericho lifted the boy's head, slid out from under him, and placed the pillow where his knee had been. He then turned to her and gestured for her to meet him out in the hallway.

She stormed away and waited while he left the room and closed the door behind him, keeping their impending argument from Gabriel's impressionable ears.

"Well?" she demanded.

Jericho winced. "I'm sorry, sweetheart—"

Dahlia smacked him on his chest in the same spot she had last night. "*Sweetheart*? Do you *want* to die?" The Voice tried to interject some reason. *You didn't seem to mind the endearment yesterday.*

"You can shut right up," Dahlia said out loud, and Jericho looked at her cautiously. Great. She was truly going crazy.

"He had a bad dream, okay?"

Dahlia reeled back. Her son had had a bad dream and gone to *Jericho*? Jealously reared its ugly head. *She* was his parent, wasn't she? What did Jericho have that she didn't?

Besides incredible height, and incredible strength, and incredible superhero looks . . .

Damn the man. No wonder her son had gone to him. He practically looked like Captain America.

The door creaked open and both Jericho and Dahlia's heads swiveled around to the sight of a sleep-rumpled little boy.

"Morning, *Mamá*, *Pa*—" Gabriel cut himself off and blushed beat red.

Red was all Dahlia was seeing. She threw her head back and groaned angrily at the ceiling. Her mind tried to tell her it was an innocent mistake—how many times do little kids call their teachers "mom" by accident—but she was having none of it.

"Your fault," she whispered at Jericho through her teeth before stalking off. She stormed through the house and right out the front door to the lawn where she sank to the ground and covered her face with her hands.

She was going to kill him. How dare he steal her son? *She* was the one who had always been there for Gabriel. And now this do-good, grinning idiot was taking her place?

Yep, she was going to kill him. But first she had to get Gabriel off to school. Without her son around, she was finally going to tear into the man.

An hour later, after Gabriel had been washed, fed, and sent off to school, Dahlia was exhausted, and the day had just begun. She was in the kitchen with Esperanza working on tamales for dinner and thinking of what she was going to say to Jericho when she heard a car pull up outside the house.

The marrow froze in her bones. She had no way of knowing this for sure, but her heart told her that trouble had finally arrived.

She'd been lulled into a sense of complacency here with Jericho taking care of everything. How had she forgotten that they would be coming for Gabriel?

She jerked her head up and her eyes immediately found Esperanza over by the stove. She had frozen in place, too. Her eyes met Dahlia's, and she read the same fear there.

Like a shot, Dahlia was out of her chair and sprinting through the living room, Esperanza right behind her. They flew to the window and glanced out surreptitiously through the curtains.

Dahlia heard the click of a pistol being cocked, and then she felt Esperanza slip the cool weight of a gun into the palm of her hand. Dahlia turned briefly to thank her and make sure the older woman was also armed before turning her attention, once again, to what was doing out in front of the house.

Dahlia's breath caught in her throat. Jericho had thrown down the tools he'd been using to repair the roof and was walking calmly to the car that idled in front of the curb. Dahlia couldn't see around him, but she could tell from the car that it was bad, but not as bad as she'd feared.

"*¿No es mi hijo?*" Esperanza asked breathlessly.

Dahlia sighed briefly and shook her head. No, it wasn't Esperanza's son. But after these clowns left, it soon would be. They were here to get information, and in her brilliance, Dahlia hadn't told Jericho all of her problem, so he may let something slip that could ruin them.

Through the haze of the curtains, Dahlia saw Jericho lean over and brace himself on the open window of the old, burgundy Lincoln and engage the occupants in conversation.

"What is he saying?" Dahlia muttered to herself, tensing as the conversation seemed to go on forever.

Like a shot, Jericho jerked from the car, took a step back, and looked over his shoulder at the house, anger flashing in his eyes.

"Oh, shit," Dahlia said at the same time Esperanza muttered, "*Madre de Dios.*"

Neither woman had a clue what had just happened, but both of them recognized infuriated male.

The Lincoln burned rubber as it pulled away from the curb, and Jericho stormed toward the house.

And just like that, everything Dahlia knew about Jericho—that he was a good man, that he would never hurt her, that she might be falling for him—fell away as Dahlia reverted about nine years into her past.

A whimper escaped her lips. One thought repeated like a mantra through her brain: *He's angry. He's angry. He's angry.*

As though under water, Dahlia heard Esperanza crooning to her, brushing her hair back from her suddenly sweat-slicked face, but Dahlia couldn't grasp what was reality, what was not.

The door of the house crashed open, bouncing off the living room wall as he barreled inside. "Dahlia!" he shouted, rage dripping from every word.

She gasped and crouched into the corner. The sound brought his head around. He spotted her.

He stomped toward her, his heavy boots eating up the floor. Dahlia couldn't breathe. Like a coward, she hid behind Esperanza, knowing he had never—*never*—hit his mother when he was like this. But Esperanza drew away from her.

He was right before her now, every muscle in her view taut with anger. He leaned over suddenly.

Dahlia's arms flew over her face, instinctively protecting the area she knew he would go for first. Sobs exploded from her chest as tears poured down her cheeks.

But the blows never came.

Her sobs finally penetrated the haze of her brain. She was crying hysterically. She peeked out through the gap in her arms to see the shell-shocked face of Jericho before her. Instead of dark, curly hair, there were blond locks over a scrunched up forehead; instead of black eyes filled with anger, ice blue eyes filled with horror.

"Does she know who I am?" he asked Esperanza brokenly, but the woman couldn't understand him, focusing instead on brushing the hair from the tear tracks on Dahlia's face.

"J-Jericho?" Dahlia asked.

All of his air left him in a whoosh, and he reached for her, jerking back the moment before contact, worry all over his face.

Dahlia realized in a second what had happened: who she thought had been coming for her, who was here before her now. She launched herself at Jericho, wrapping her arms around his neck and burying her face in his chest while she shuddered, shaking away the weight of the past's nightmares.

Jericho moved them both until he was sitting with his back against the wall, Dahlia clutched firmly to his front and settled on his lap. "Shh, sweetheart," he whispered to her over and over again. It was then that Dahlia realized she was hyperventilating.

"I c-can't stop it," she gasped, panic rising again, mostly at the fact that her body had run completely out of control on her.

Lightly, Jericho cupped his hand over her nose and gasping mouth, leaving much space between his palm and her face. It created the bag effect she had seen on television so many times. Immediately, her senses were flooded with Jericho's scent mixed with the outdoor smells of grass and lumber. She calmed down in an instant.

As soon as Jericho noticed her breathing was regulating, he dropped his hand and used both of his arms to crush her to him. "I'm sorry," he whispered into her hair. "So sorry that I scared you."

She pulled back to look at his face and was shocked to see his blue eyes brimming with tears.

"You will tell me who taught you to be afraid like that," he growled, "and I will kill him."

Dahlia could tell from the grim look of him that Jericho meant every word. And with all her heart, she wanted nothing else than for him to slay this dragon for her.

"Gabriel's father," she whispered.

He nodded, obviously already arrived at that conclusion.

But she knew he hadn't guessed this next part: "My husband," she said so softly she wondered if he'd heard her, if she'd have to repeat the hated words again.

His face blanched. "Your . . . *husband?*"

She buried her face in his chest and nodded against the t-shirt fabric. She cinched her lips shut, afraid that it was all going to come tumbling out of her now that she'd opened the floodgates even just this much.

"You're married," he said, like a man facing the gallows.

Dahlia expected him to shove her away, expected his wholesome nature to end their relationship right this second, so when he pulled her even closer and shuddered out a sigh, she closed her eyes in relief. He wasn't rejecting her. And the fact that that had been Dahlia's greatest fear jolted her upright.

She cared for Jericho. Maybe even . . . *loved* him.

"Oh, no," she mumbled.

"What?" Jericho asked anxiously.

"No, no, no." This couldn't be happening. Where was her much-needed distance? How was she going to survive when he left her? They always left. Sometimes they hit and left, but the leaving part was a constant.

"Dahlia," Jericho said in a firm voice. "Just tell me what's going on. We can fix it, whatever it is."

"Damn it, stop saying stuff like that to me!" Even Dahlia could tell that her tone was bordering on unhinged. She took a huge breath and held it in her lungs for several seconds before letting it out along with some of her anxious tension. "Okay, okay," she said to all three of them in the room. Esperanza had moved to Jericho's side and was watching her through eyes that rivaled Jericho's on the wariness level. "Yes, I'm married," she began, "but I haven't seen my . . . husband," the word was hard to spit out, "in nine years. Not since I found out I was pregnant and ran like hell."

The anger made a reappearance in Jericho's stance and expression. "He hit you." It wasn't a question, but Dahlia nodded her head anyway.

"I'm going to kill him," Jericho said for the second time, and he began pacing the room.

"I never told him about Gabriel," Dahlia said loudly to be heard over Jericho's muttering.

"Good," he breathed in relief.

"No, not good," Dahlia immediately countered. "Because he found out, and now he's coming for Gabriel to take him . . . a-away from me." She knew she was perilously close to losing it again, so she closed her eyes and tried to regulate her breathing. But with the new wave of calm came a terrifying thought. Her eyes flew open. "Gabriel's at school," she blurted, panic dripping from every syllable.

Jericho turned to her. In a second, she saw the implication flash through his eyes. Gabriel was at school—the only elementary school in a ten-mile radius. He was a tiny sitting duck, and those fuckers in the Lincoln were probably on orders to grab-and-go.

Gabriel might even now be gone from her forever.

Chapter Twelve

Jericho felt all of the blood leave his head. "No," he muttered, images of those men from the car kidnapping Gabriel and taking him away forever spurring him over to Dahlia and hauling her to her feet.

"Let's go. Now," he said shortly and started sprinting out of the house with Dahlia right behind him. They launched themselves into the truck, and Jericho threw it into gear and sped off in the direction of the school.

"No, no, *no*," she chanted continuously as Jericho sped through the neighborhood. He could hear her frantic breaths and knew she was hyperventilating again. The panic Jericho was feeling was almost debilitating, and this was not even his son they were driving toward. He couldn't imagine what she must be feeling.

As they approached the school, Jericho noticed that it was recess time; all of the children were out in the fenced-in yard. It was the perfect blend of chaos to hide a kidnapping. Those men could have been in and out with Gabriel without anyone noticing.

As soon as the truck stopped, they both shot themselves out of the truck and toward the yard. Dahlia didn't slow once she reached the yard. She launched herself through the mass of tiny bodies, slowing down only enough to make sure she didn't hurt any children.

"Gabriel," Dahlia yelled at the top of her lungs. Jericho could tell immediately that the boy would never be able to hear her over the similar din from the kids.

"Gabriel!" he bellowed as he moved in front of Dahlia and pulled her through the path the kids made as they spied a speeding giant. He got them to the flagpole where he gave Dahlia a boost and helped her shimmy up. Now they were both at a good height for spotting Gabriel.

Jericho saw him first. "Over there," he shouted over his shoulder as he set off to the corner of the school building where he'd spotted Gabriel playing over by a bike rack. Dahlia was clinging to the back of his t-shirt as Jericho—like a man possessed—sprinted toward the boy.

As soon as they broke free from the crush of bodies, Dahlia shot around Jericho and ran the remaining steps to her son, scooping him up into her arms with a sob and hugging him as hard as she could.

Jericho stepped behind her without thought and put his arms around them both, breathing a quick "Thank God."

Dahlia lifted her head from where it had been buried in the boy's grubby neck to look at Jericho. An odd emotion was reflected there—something Jericho couldn't put his finger on, but knew he himself was feeling.

"Thank you," she whispered to him. And then, she reached one arm around his neck and pulled him close for a brief, scorching kiss.

*

Gabriel was still crushed into a hug between their two bodies, and Dahlia could feel his curious little eyes on them as she quickly and fiercely kissed Jericho.

What would she have done without him?

She pulled back slightly. They were still close enough that their breaths fanned each other's faces, close enough for her to see the abject relief in his eyes. Relief that they had found Gabriel; that Gabriel was alive and safe.

Why did he care?

And why didn't she want to examine his motives more closely? She was just simply grateful for his help and for his presence. In this moment in time, with Gabriel in her arms and Jericho's blue eyes focused on her, she couldn't imagine anywhere else she wanted to be—anyone else she wanted to be with.

"Shh, everything's okay now," Jericho whispered to her, lifting a thumb to her face and wiping a tear she hadn't realized was trailing down her cheek.

"Mommy?" Gabriel asked in a soft, scared voice.

Dahlia wished she had herself together enough to reassure her son, let him know everything was okay, but she was too overwhelmed. After a few seconds, Jericho saved her. "It's okay, buddy," he said gently, ruffling the boy's hair. "She just really missed you and wanted to see you."

Dahlia watched as, like magic, the fear disappeared from Gabriel's eyes and he turned a sunny smile upon her. If Jericho said things were okay, Gabriel believed him.

"Let's get you both home, hmmm?" he asked gently.

Dahlia felt herself nodding numbly, and she turned to walk back toward the truck. She made it two steps before her knees buckled beneath her. Before she could fall and hurt both herself and her son, Jericho caught her with an arm around her waist. Once she was steady again, he scooped Gabriel from her arms. The boy latched to him like a monkey—arms tight around Jericho's neck, legs no doubt squeezing his ribs painfully—and she watched as Jericho murmured something to him that she couldn't hear.

Jericho turned toward her and offered her the hand that wasn't supporting Gabriel. She watched in slow motion as her hand moved toward his. He closed the remaining distance and threaded their fingers together, giving them a warm squeeze. "Let's go," he said, and began a slow trek back to the parking lot. They paused briefly as Jericho had a whispered conversation with the playground attendant, and then they were in the truck.

On the return trip, Dahlia simply held her son and breathed in his little-boy scent of grass and dirt. When Jericho parked the truck in front of the house, he walked around the truck and opened the passenger door, helping Gabriel to the ground and then reaching for her and helping her to the ground as well. He whispered something to Gabriel again, and he scampered off into the house.

Once he was out of sight, the remaining strength she had been clutching to her soul like a suit of armor finally chipped. She covered her face with both hands and let the tears flow.

She was a failure. She was here because Gabriel was in danger, and she hadn't been able to keep him safe to start with. And now? Now they were worse off than they'd ever been.

Strong arms came around her and pulled her close to a warm, wide chest. "Let it go, sweetheart." The words rumbled from Jericho's chest and through to the center of her grief. "Let it go. There's no one here to see you, and you deserve a good cry."

She knew that wasn't true. Dahlia didn't deserve anything, but damned if she could refuse such a tempting offer. Her hands moved from their crushed space between his chest and her face to his back. She clutched at him, unable to relax her fingers from their desperate hold, pinching the muscles covering his upper back. He just held her, breathing steadily into the hair above her ear, rubbing her back in circles.

When she was finally able to get ahold of her own body, she forced herself to stop crying. She couldn't afford any signs of weakness, and she knew if she didn't stop up this dam of tears, she would cry for quite possibly the rest of her life. She pulled back and attempted to step out of the circle of his arms, but he held her fast. Those long fingers of his came under her chin and tipped her face up. She refused to look at him, lowering her eyes until— damn it—all she could see was that delectable mouth. At least it distracted her from the turmoil of emotions she was battling.

"Look at me," he whispered.

Reluctantly, she raised her eyes to his, and once they arrived at their destination, she sucked in a breath. She'd never seen this expression on a man's face before. Reflected in his eyes was a heart-stopping blend of caring, reassurance, promise, even lust.

"I will fix this for you," he promised solemnly.

Dahlia felt her eyes widen. *What?*

"We'll stay," he continued. "As long as I can hold them off, we'll stay." The firm hold he had on her chin turned into a caress, and she couldn't stop herself from leaning her cheek into his hand. "We'll make sure Gabriel is safe, and then we'll decide what to do next." He nodded as though he hadn't an idea that he was going to say what he'd just said, but he fully supported his own decision, and Dahlia felt an unwelcome sense of dread in the pit of her stomach.

Oh, God, he should have never said that. She could never un-hear that, could never forget the gratefulness that had flared immediately at his words. Gratefulness and something else. Something she was going to just shove to the back of the clusterfuck that was her current emotional state. Men who abused her, used her, left her—that she could handle. This?

How in God's name was she going to keep her distance from him now?

Chapter Thirteen

Jericho and Dahlia had formed a quick plan. It involved getting the house ready to put on the market tomorrow so they could get Gabriel into a new house as soon as possible. While Jericho worked on making the roof inspection-ready, the women were inside scrubbing the house from top to bottom. It was taking all of Jericho's willpower to not just buy them a house outright and get Gabriel moved to a safer location tonight. But, he knew instinctively that Dahlia would resent it. Even with that hanging over his head, Jericho still wasn't sure he was going to be able to hold himself back. Only the knowledge that he could and would protect Dahlia and Gabriel from any threat kept him sane.

Gabriel was following Jericho around like a lost puppy in the front yard, and if he didn't stop soon, Jericho was pretty sure his heart was going to bleed right out of his chest.

God, how was he ever going to be strong enough to get through this? Gabriel was the perfect eight-year-old boy. Full of orneriness, love for his mama, and now hero worship for him.

The worst part of it all was that Gabriel's constant presence was, for the first time since Jericho had watched his mate die, pushing the pain of his own child's loss into the background.

Jericho stumbled over his own feet in the front yard where he was moving debris from the roof into a pile. He realized with horror that this was the first time he'd so much as thought about his family in—

When *was* the last time he'd thought about his family?

Jericho waited for the onrush of guilt at betraying his mate and child. He waited. And waited. He stood still so long that Gabriel looked up at him from where he had been playing with rocks by the debris pile.

Jericho finally had to admit that, other than a slight niggle, he did not feel guilty. For anything—not what he'd done with Dahlia the past couple of days, not for falling fast for a bright-eyed little boy.

Something had changed between them. Jericho knew he was not the kind of man who could get involved in a physical relationship with a woman and have it mean nothing to him. He'd had one lover in his life, and when he had made love to Emily for the first time, it had bonded them body *and* soul. It only made sense that his actions with Dahlia would have the same effect.

But then, what had happened this morning with Dahlia had bonded them as well. His protective instincts had roared to full life. Rage that anyone was threatening the safety of his mate and her child—he had no words for the depth of that emotion. And now, he wanted Dahlia so badly he couldn't see straight.

Gabriel rocketed to his feet and bounded toward Jericho. "What's next, Jericho?" he asked in that childish, slightly accented voice.

Jericho couldn't stop himself from grinning down at the boy and ruffling his hair. "Same old, same old, buddy. We need to keep moving all the junk in your yard to this pile." He nodded toward the growing pile of shingles, rotted timber, and other extraneous pieces of construction.

The little boy's shoulders slumped slightly as his bright eyes took in all they still had to do in the front yard. They hadn't even begun to tackle the backyard. Jericho knew he had to be bored. "Hey, why don't you go help your mama in the house? I bet she could use a man to do some heavy lifting for her."

Gabriel straightened with an air of importance. "Okay," he said gravely before sprinting through the yard and into the house.

Jericho watched him go with not a small amount of sadness. The boy's presence had brightened Jericho's work. But Dahlia would benefit from having him close more than Jericho would.

Her tears this afternoon had broken his heart. No one had to tell him how strong of a woman she was. That she had lost it as she had was pretty glaring evidence that life was giving her a little too much to handle right now.

Whatever Jericho could do to lighten the load, he would do.

For the next several hours, Jericho worked through the front and back yards, gathering all of the rubble. By the time the sun went down, he was tired, he was sweaty, and his hands felt like they'd been ripped to shreds, even though he wore thick gardening gloves.

Oh well. The one thing Jericho knew for sure was that any pain was temporary. He peeled off the gloves and ran a quick inspection over his fingers and palms. The blisters were already healing. In the next hour or so, they'd be completely gone.

He headed toward the front door, excitement coursing through him that he would be seeing Dahlia and Gabriel again. He was a little worried that he seemed to have missed them. He was still going to have to take Dahlia back to the compound eventually. What would he do when his actions caused her to hate him? He missed her after a couple of hours apart while on the same property. What if she refused to ever see him again?

His gait quickened, and when he ducked through the low threshold, his eyes found Dahlia immediately. She and Esperanza were still in the middle of the deep-clean of their house. Jericho spotted Gabriel with the broom—the handle towered over his head—at the same time that Gabriel spotted him.

"Jericho," he crowed joyfully, dropping the broom and zooming over. He skidded to a stop right in front of Jericho and shifted his weight back and forth on both feet self-consciously. Some unknown instinct informed Jericho that the kid was trying not to hug him. Jericho raised one arm slightly, and it was all the invitation Gabriel needed. He scooted under Jericho's arm and wrapped his dust and dirt caked arms around Jericho's waist tightly, burying his face in Jericho's ribs.

Jericho closed his eyes slightly as he fought to swallow past his suddenly swollen Adam's apple. "Hey, bud," he said on a croak. "Good work in here. Looks almost good as new."

Gabriel beamed up at him. Dahlia's stomach growled—Jericho heard it from all the way across the room—and Jericho's eyes flew to her face. She was watching Gabriel and Jericho warily and absently rubbing her stomach.

"Supper time," Jericho said, looking at Gabriel once more. "Want to go with me to pick up some food, little man?"

He should have thought of food earlier. He knew that the women had been working on tamales earlier in the day, but the excitement of Gabriel's predicament and then their hasty decision to sell the house had distracted them. Now Dahlia was hungry enough that her stomach was roaring. Guilt assuaged Jericho again. He needed to take better care of her.

"Sure," Gabriel said.

Jericho raised questioning eyes to Dahlia, who jerked herself out of deep thought once she realized he was looking at her. "That sounds great, thank you," she whispered to him.

Jericho knew Gabriel and Esperanza were watching, but he walked over to Dahlia to briefly trail his fingers down her cheek. "Doing okay?" he asked for her ears only.

She jerked anxiously away from his touch and nodded like a bobblehead. Jericho frowned for a second before carefully schooling his expression. Apparently they'd lost some ground since earlier.

That was okay. They'd been apart. She'd had time to freak out and think everything was a mistake. Jericho could work to regain some of that lost ground.

"We'll be back soon," he said to her, loud enough for everyone to hear. "I'll keep him safe," he tacked on in a whisper.

Gratefulness flared in her eyes briefly. "Thank you."

"Okay, Gabe, let's go," Jericho said, turning around and heading toward the door. He could hear the over-exuberant slap of Gabriel's tennis shoes on the ground behind him as they exited the house and walked toward the truck.

"Jericho, can we get Happy Meals?" Gabriel asked as Jericho buckled him in.

"Happy Meals?" Jericho asked. Would Dahlia kill him if he got Gabriel junk food?

"Yeah. Mom needs a Happy Meal so she gets happier."

Sound logic. "Yeah, sure, bud, we can get Happy Meals. That's a great idea."

Twenty minutes later, bogged down with two Happy Meals for everyone, they were returning to the house. Jericho had to admit he'd had more fun on this little excursion than he could remember ever having. The kid was keeping up a constant litany of pointless jabber, and Jericho was hanging on his every word.

Kids were so . . . *neat*. How had he missed that memo? Jericho had mourned the loss of his own child for eight years, but if he'd have known he was missing this magic, he'd have been even more inconsolable than he had been.

God, how did Dahlia stay away from him?

Guilt flared. He was going to be taking her away from him again. He felt blood rush to his neck and face. That didn't sit well. Those were his orders, but he wasn't sure he could follow them anymore. A new plan began to formulate, and for the first time in years, Jericho felt hope.

They arrived back at the house, and Jericho followed an exuberant Gabriel into the house, his arms laden with bags of food.

"We're home!" Gabriel announced to the empty living room.

Jericho couldn't prevent the flare of warmth the boy's innocent words caused. Oh, if only—

"That was fast," Dahlia said, coming around the corner quickly and a little anxiously. She had obviously worried about Gabriel while they had been gone. "And you brought . . . McDonalds." Her eyes found Jericho's and she raised an eyebrow.

Yup, he'd been right. Dahlia was not a fan of feeding her son junk. Jericho shrugged with one shoulder and tried to prevent a grin. Dahlia was pretty cute when she was piqued.

"Happy Meals," Gabriel announced importantly.

"Oh," Dahlia said, shooting Jericho another look, this one asking *Um . . . what?*

"To make you happier," Jericho said softly. Gabriel nodded.

"Ah," Dahlia flat-out grinned, and Jericho heard himself suck in a breath. Damn, she was amazingly beautiful. "Now, that is a genius idea, *mijo*," she told Gabriel, striding over to him, swinging him up and planting a noisy, wet kiss on his cheek. "Go wash your hands and get *abuelita*. She's in your room."

She gave Jericho a shy smile and gestured for him to take the food into the kitchen. He couldn't wait to let her know the plan he'd come up with.

*

Dinner was quick and mostly silent. They were all exhausted from the labor of the day. As soon as Gabriel finished his chicken nuggets and bounded off to play, Dahlia felt despair filter in again. "I can't lose him," she whispered.

"That is not going to happen," Jericho said with authority. "Not today, not ever, do you understand me?"

Dahlia shook her head. "Luis will have help. I've never been able to win against him. He wants Gabriel, he will take him, and I won't be able to do anything about it."

"Yeah, well, *I* want Gabriel," Jericho said, still calmly, but Dahlia reeled back. "And I want you. You're all my family now," he said, leaning back to include Esperanza. "And I won't ever let anyone take my family away from me again." He leaned forward to press a swift kiss to her lips. "I love you, Dahlia."

"*Shit!*" Dahlia screeched. "Are you kidding me with this?" she asked the ceiling, tossing her hands up in the air.

"Wrong answer," Jericho said, and then he scooped Dahlia up

with an arm beneath her knees and behind her back and carried her down the hall while she sputtered in disbelief.

"Where are we going?" she asked as she wiggled to get down.

His firm grip tightened even more. "Somewhere private."

She felt no fear at his words, but she did feel panic. No, she couldn't be alone with him. Not after he'd just offered to fix her world for her. Oh, yeah, and thrown in the love thing. No, she definitely could not be alone with him, because the moment the door closed, she was going to jump his bones.

And then the door closed. Jericho stepped inside Dahlia's bedroom and kicked the door closed with his foot, not even pausing in his stride to her bed. He dumped her unceremoniously onto the top, and she bounced a good two feet before landing. In a flash, Jericho dove on top of her, pinning her with his weight. He slid one thigh between her legs and brought his hands up to her face. One set of fingers dove into her hair, the other languorously brushed across her lower lip. Back and forth, back and forth.

"Now," he said in a soft, low voice. "You're the bravest woman I know. Earlier today, you were holding a gun, ready to go to battle for your son. You're a fierce and strong fighter." Dahlia opened her mouth to protest, remembering with shame how completely she'd lost it while huddled in the corner of the living room mere hours ago, but he cut her off. "Just what is it about me—about *us*—that scares you so much?"

Scared? Of a relationship with Jericho? Try debilitatingly terrified. The idea was completely abhorrent to her. Letting another man close enough to her to hurt her? To make her fall in love with him and then watch, devastated, as he walked away?

Never again.

But did he need to know all of that? Self-preservation was Dahlia's greatest learned instinct. "I'm not scared." There was no way he was going to buy that. Her voice had wavered.

He smiled at her briefly. "Okay, then." And he swooped down

and kissed her. Thoroughly. He didn't have to wait for her lips to part, they did automatically, but then he completely infiltrated her. His tongue swept into her mouth, teasing, tasting. His hands moved, one to cup the back of her head and hold her more firmly against his onslaught, the other to trail down her neck, leaving licks of fire, over her collarbone, and down to cup her breast.

She cried out, and his mouth absorbed the sound. He made a low, encouraging noise in the back of his throat, and deepened the kiss even further. He sucked her tongue back into his own mouth, nibbled on her lower lip, fisted his hand in her hair.

He seemed to be everywhere at once. A million different sensations, and all of them swept her away. Her hands, where they had been fastidiously fisted at her sides, uncoiled and rose to clutch him to her. She could feel him smile against her lips.

He pulled back. "Hmm." His tongue swept his glistening lower lip and then he sucked it into his mouth and nibbled on it, drawing every last taste of her lips from his own.

Dahlia's mouth fell open and a whimper escaped. She'd never seen anyone do that before, never had that effect on anyone. It made her want to lean forward and chew on his lip for him. She was leaning forward to do just that, but he pulled back when she neared. She frowned at him.

He shook his head, an obnoxious crooked smile spread his face. "Not yet." His hand rose from her breast to her face where his fingertips brushed over her lips. "How do you feel about me?"

She jerked her head away from his fingers. Oh, that's how he was going to play this? Tease a confession of love—or whatever, she mentally corrected herself—out of her by teasing her libido? "That's fine. I wasn't really into this anyway," she lied—blatantly apparently, as his grin just got wider.

Jericho raised one eyebrow, and then his fingers left her lips, trailed back down her neck over her collarbone. Dahlia felt her back arch to meet his touch, already anticipating the thrill of his hand on her breast.

Jericho chuckled. "Not into it, hmm?" he asked while tracking a circle around her aching nipple with one finger.

"Fine," she snapped, embarrassed. "I'm into it, but I don't want to have this conversation!"

"Shh," he whispered. "I know, sweetheart. But *I* want to have this conversation," he said earnestly, his eyes sparking. "I want to tell you how I feel about you, and yes, I want to know how you feel about me. I need to hear it."

She could feel her frown deepening. "Sure you need to hear it, so you can use it against me later." Now, how had that slipped out? She definitely hadn't meant to have said that, and she could tell by the look on Jericho's face that he wasn't going to just let it slide.

"Use it against you?" he muttered. And then the next second, he had her gathered in his arms, crushing her with his whole body weight that was no longer supported by his elbows. "Dahlia, sweet, what has been done to you," he was muttering next to her ear.

She closed her eyes. His reaction was shaking her. Either he was a damn good actor, or he was legitimately worried about her and cared for her. Neither was something she craved.

He pulled back to look in her eyes, and the pure, blue color sucked her in. She felt her breath hitch. One of his hands came up between their bodies to lay over his heart. "I will *never* use your feelings for me against you," he whispered fervently. "Believe what I'm telling you. *Never*," he repeated.

The Knowledge spread reverberations of Jericho's goodness throughout her body, leaving no question as to his sincerity. He was telling the truth, and that was a new concept to Dahlia—well, new relatively. Jericho always seemed to tell her the truth . . .

In fact, Jericho seemed to always do just what she needed.

"I'm crazy about you," she whispered.

Out loud.

"Damn it!" She slapped a hand over her mouth. Had she really just said that out loud? She braced herself and looked into Jericho's eyes, knowing she would see triumph. But she didn't.

Jericho's eyes had gone soft. His smile was no longer borderline sarcastic, but warm and to a lesser scale. What was worse is he didn't say anything. No, "I knew it," or "Hope you don't mind one-sided relationships." He just smiled at her.

It made Dahlia uncomfortable enough to squirm. After what seemed to be years of waiting, Jericho finally said, "Thank you, sweetheart. You don't know how happy that made me." And then before she could say or do anything else or even react to that unexpected response, he dipped his head and placed his lips against hers achingly gently.

Unexpectedly, tears sprang to her eyes and her breath hitched in her throat. She was shocked to realize that she didn't regret saying the words, even though they had slipped out unbidden.

Jericho pulled back from the kiss, gazed deeply into her eyes, and said, "Come back with me."

Dahlia gasped in shock. "What?"

"Come back with me. You and Gabriel and Esperanza. You need protection, and I can give it to you. We'll go back to the facility. I've thought about it all evening. It's a way to follow orders *and* follow my heart," Jericho said in a rush, obviously desperate to get the words out. "I need you, sweetheart. I need you and Gabriel, and I think you both need me."

Dahlia gaped at him in complete shock. Never in her life would she have guessed he would offer this to her. And she was so tempted to take it—take what he was offering—and run with him into the sunset. She wanted it so badly.

She could never have it. Dahlia and men—they just didn't go together.

To distract him from what he'd just done, from the words that had thrown her world into upheaval, she pulled him back down and fitted his lips to hers. She couldn't tell him no yet. She had to have him at least once. It was damned selfish of her, but then, that was her MO, wasn't it?

Jericho deepened the kiss with obvious joy, taking her kiss as an answer and sweeping his tongue into her mouth. He nudged her legs apart with his knee, and when she moved, he settled deeply into the space between her thighs, lying flush against her. Her breasts were crushed by his chest; his rigid abdomen was cradled by her softer stomach. Immediately, all thought of what she had said, what he had said, disappeared. The Impulse took over. All Dahlia could think of was that she *needed* Jericho badly. More than she'd ever needed anything in her life. They'd been Impulse-paired for three days, and both of them had worked valiantly to delay this innate need they each felt to consummate their desire for each other. Apparently, the Impulse would be delayed no longer.

As though reading her thoughts, Jericho groaned in the back of his throat and his kiss grew more urgent. His arms tightened around her, drawing her closer to the center of his being, and she felt him begin to rock his hips into her, thrusting softly.

By the shaking of his body, she could tell he was holding back. But she wanted the out-of-control lover that Jericho had shown her he would be in all of their previous encounters. "Let go," she whispered, and his body jolted at her words. "Don't hold back, please." She was shocked at the desperation in her voice.

He moaned. "Don't—" he cut off to kiss her brutally again and pulled back violently. "Don't say that. I can't control it if you say things like that." Already, his thrusts had grown firmer, the bed creaking beneath them with his movement.

Her hands flew to his ass, her nails digging into the denim

covering the muscle she wanted to feel flesh-to-flesh. "Yes, just like that," she said breathlessly.

"God," she thought she heard him utter, and then he broke.

He roughly kicked her legs further apart, rising to his knees between her thighs, allowing his hips to swing down freely to drive against her center again and again. His pace increased; he buried his face in her neck, and she felt him bite down on her throat hard enough to sting so sweetly. She cried out and raised her hands to his back, running her fingers beneath his shirt, her nails scraping his skin.

"Dahlia," he gasped. "Please stop me. I don't want to hurt you."

Oh, God. "You're not hurting me," she moaned as he licked away the sting from his bite. She heard a pounding right above her head, and glanced up quickly to see that Jericho's fist had found the headboard. The smooth oak was marred by a fist-shaped indentation, and now Jericho's red, scraped knuckles were blanching white as he gripped the top of the headboard in a death-hold.

"I need you," he moaned into her damp skin. "*Now.* I need you now."

She could only manage a moan in response, which luckily he took as assent. He shoved off of the headboard to kneel between her legs. His hands flew to her fly without finesse, and her hands joined his, hurting more than helping in their combined frenzy to get her pants off. With an exasperated gasp, she moved her hands to his jeans, tugging until the button came free. At the same moment that he finally got her pants open and tugged them down her thighs in rough jerks, Dahlia slipped her hand inside his jeans and wrapped her hand around his velvety erection.

He hissed through his teeth, throwing his head back. The cords of his neck stood out in stark relief, and Dahlia shoved herself up with her free hand until she was at a level where she could lick up to his jaw from his collarbone. She nibbled near the dimple of his chin.

Like a shot, Jericho was off the bed. He reached down and pulled Dahlia's pants the rest of the way off and then unceremoniously shucked his own and drew his shirt over his head, tossing it to the floor. Dahlia caught breathtaking glimpses of smooth, pale skin clinging to mouthwatering muscles before he leaned down again and grasped the bottom of her shirt. "I want to see all of you, sweetheart," he whispered, whisking her shirt over her head.

And then he abruptly stopped. He froze like a deer in the headlights. His eyes hazed with passion further as he looked at her spread on the bed below him. His erection kicked violently, and his hand came to his chest, rubbing in a circle absently while his gaze swept from the crown of her head to her toes and then back again.

Knowing she was teasing him, Dahlia arched her back, thrusting her breasts into the air while he watched. His expression grew pained for a nanosecond, and then he leapt at her. Dahlia gasped as his body weight drove all the air out of her body. He landed between her legs, lunged forward to kiss her, thrusting his tongue into her mouth. She felt his fingers brush down her outer thigh, grab behind her knee, and push her leg up until her knee was at his ribcage. She felt the blunt head of his erection prod her entrance. He tossed his head back. His grip on her leg grew almost unbearably rough, and then he thrust into her in one brutal movement, seating himself to the hilt, his hips grinding against hers.

They cried out at the same time. Dahlia didn't know if she was crying out from pain or from pleasure. She'd been ready for him, aching for him, but his invasion of her body had been brutal. He was large, uncomfortable. Glorious.

"I'm hurting you," he ground out, his teeth clenched. "Sweet, I'm sorry. I'm trying to stop." His entire body was shaking. His abdominal muscles were clenching and unclenching viciously as he tried to stop himself from thrusting into her and didn't quite succeed. His hips jerked against hers. He moaned, a desperate sound part pain, part supplication. Her name fell from his lips in a breathless entreaty.

Her body responded to the sight in a rush of moisture. He was the sexiest sight she'd ever seen, and his inability to control his reaction to her turned her on to no end. She brought her hands to his chest, stroking the sweat-slicked skin briefly before exerting pressure, pushing him down to the bed. In an instant, he wrapped his arms around her and flipped over to his back while simultaneously making sure he never left her body, placing her firmly above him.

She straddled his hips, rose on her knees, and sank down on him slightly. She sighed in relief. She was better able to control the penetration from this position, and all traces of pain disappeared.

In a brief moment of clarity, Dahlia glanced down at Jericho spread beneath her. She groaned. His pale skin was glistening with sweat. His wide chest heaved up and down and was framed by his arms, bulging in the restraint he exerted over himself and the death-grip he had on the sheets by her knees. His abdomen trembled, muscles shivering as they clenched over and over, creating stark lines of shadow between each ridge of muscle. Her eyes flew to his face, traveling up his heavily corded neck, to find that his head was kicked back, his eyes clenched shut and his teeth smashed together as he hissed in and out through parted lips.

Her heart stuttered. He was trying so hard to hold back, to treat her gently. Tenderly. She leaned forward, sprawling her hands on his chest, to place a kiss on the corner of his mouth.

He forced his eyes open, a slight panic evident in their depths, and looked at her. "I'm sorry . . . didn't mean . . . to hurt—"

She cut him off with another kiss, this one full on his mouth, invading him by forcing her tongue through his teeth. She moaned in encouragement when he tentatively kissed her back, and then followed up the moan with a swivel of her hips, taking him deeper inside her body.

He broke away from the kiss to cry out, and his hips jerked below hers, thrusting himself the rest of the way.

This time, though, it didn't hurt. "Yes," Dahlia moaned desperately. "Jericho . . . do it again."

His eyes found hers again, locking in on her gaze as he withdrew and thrust again. This time it was her head that kicked back, her teeth that clenched, her breath that billowed in and out of her body.

"Oh, God," he groaned, repeating the action and picking up speed. "Sweetheart, I'm not going . . . to last—" he cut off with another groan.

She barely heard him. Her body was galloping toward the edge of her pleasure and the world was tunneling. She pushed up, off of his chest and sat atop him to ride him hard. He grunted in the back of his throat with each of her movements.

She reached down and snatched his hands, which were still fisted in the sheets, and moved them to her breasts, spreading them over the taut peaks and holding them there with her hands over his. Guiding his fingers, he encouraged her to pinch her nipples, and when he did, she made a noise close to a scream and heard him echo the sentiment.

He raised his knees, digging his heels into the bed beneath them and thrusting with more strength. She leaned back against the corded muscle of his thighs, unable to control her frenzied movement this close to the end. One of his hands left her breast, trailing down her stomach. His thumb found her clit. He circled it once, and Dahlia came apart.

Her body snapped so tightly, she couldn't scream his name like she wanted to. It came out closer to a whimper. Between her straining thighs, she felt Jericho's body tense, and then she felt the first hot jet deep inside her as he followed her over.

"God . . . Dahlia . . . love you," he gasped, his hips bucking uncontrollably.

And to her shock, she heard herself whisper it back to him as she came down from the stars.

Chapter Fourteen

Jericho was in heaven. Heaven at this current moment was Dahlia, still straddling him, sprawled across his chest. Her breath was coming in sweet puffs against the damp skin of his neck. One of his hands clutched her perfect ass. The other was playing with her hair, threading his fingers through it, then drawing his hand away and watching as the silk sifted through his fingers, catching the starlight that streamed in through the window in a wide array of colors.

He was still buried blissfully deeply inside of her, and very quickly, she was going to be able to tell that he was up for round two.

She'd told him that she loved him.

He was still grinning like an idiot over that—well, that and the mind-blowing love they'd just made. The best of his life, which, he realized, wasn't saying much given his inexperience, but instinctually, he knew what they'd done was not the usual romp in the hay everyone raved about.

He also knew that she'd avoided responding to his new plan. He wasn't an idiot. But all of him hoped that she would recognize the need behind the plan. As long as Luis—that fucker—was alive, Gabriel and Dahlia were in danger. She loved her son too much to put him in danger, just so she could have her freedom. Right? He hoped.

She sighed in his arms, and Jericho was pretty sure he'd never been this content. Not even with Emily. Granted, he'd already known Dahlia longer than he'd been in love with Emily, but still. Emily had been his first—his only—for the last eight years. She had been perfect, sweet, adorable. Compared to Dahlia, they were like night and day. Emily the light, Dahlia the dark, seductive night.

And he wondered now how he'd ever thought he would be happy with anything other than what Dahlia brought to the table. Even when making love to Emily the few times they had, he'd never lost control with her like he had just looking at Dahlia's bare body. Emily had inspired a calm in him; Dahlia threw him out of his mind.

And he felt a twinge of guilt that he preferred the chaos to what he would have had with his first mate.

He was unable to hold his lust at bay any longer. His raging erection twitched inside Dahlia, and her head snapped up. A slow, lazy smile spread across her face and she winked at him before lowering her head to place a gentle kiss to his lips.

As soon as their lips touched, Jericho lost it—again. He flipped them over, settling between her spread thighs and thrusting in a slow rhythm while he deepened their kiss.

"Mmm . . . *baby*," she gasped against his lips as her hips joined his. "You feel so good." She moaned again. "Like there's nothing between us."

He smiled down at her, but only for a second because she suddenly froze, her eyes widening in horror. Jericho froze, too, unsure what had just happened.

With superhuman strength, Dahlia pushed Jericho away from her. He reluctantly withdrew from her body, and her eyes flew down to look at his glistening erection.

"Oh, *shit*," she said softly.

His eyes followed hers down to where she was gaping, expecting to find . . . he wasn't sure what. He relaxed in relief to see everything was still attached where it was supposed to be. He looked at her again, confused.

"Where's the condom?" she asked, panic in her voice, panic that finally found its way into Jericho's brain.

His chest seized. He could feel his eyes stretching as wide as saucers. Oh, God, he'd done it again. He might have just gotten her pregnant. His baby would kill her. He'd lose her—

All the air he needed rushed into his lungs as he remembered a vital detail. "Hey," he crooned to her wildly writhing form as she tried to get out from under him. "It's okay. You've eaten the fruit, remember?"

Instead of calming her like he'd thought, she fought harder, smacking his chest—a habit of hers apparently—with an open palm until he moved back and let her up. "You think I'm worried about *dying*?" she screeched as she frantically looked around the floor for her clothing.

Jericho tried not to focus on the way her body moved as she bent over to pick up her pants and shirt. "Aren't you?" he asked.

"No, you ass! I'm worried about bringing another child into this world—by myself!" She jerked her shirt over her head with violent movements and then stepped into her jeans.

Jericho relaxed completely. "No worries," he told her. "We'll get married." It was the part of the plan he hadn't shared with her yet. No time like the present.

She froze in the process of buttoning her jeans. Slowly, her head came up. The look in her eyes froze the blood in his veins. Every spark of affection was absent from her usually warm brown eyes. Her face was a hardened mask. "Married?" she said in a low voice. "Are you fucking kidding me?"

She stalked toward him where he sat on the bed, and he had to resist the urge to scoot away from her as she neared. "I'm already married, remember?" She flung the words in his face. "To an asshole who beat me, knocked me up, and is now after my son."

Jericho had nothing to say to that. Somehow, *But I love you*, seemed grossly inadequate. She didn't wait for him to say anything anyway, spinning on her heel and stomping away from him toward the door.

He was losing her. His frantic mind screamed at him for action, and he was out of the bed before he had the time to think it through. He sprinted across the bedroom and caught her just in front of the door. He gathered her into his arms, pulling her back against his front, and buried his face in her hair. She immediately struggled against his hold, but he stilled her movements easily. "Shh," he whispered. "Dahlia, stop and think. We're an Impulse pair. We can't live without each other." She snorted. "Okay, I can't live without you," he corrected. "I love you, sweetheart."

She stopped struggling and seemed to deflate in his arms. He gathered her closer, pressed a kiss to the back of her neck. "That's what you all say," she whispered in a defeated voice.

"This is different, and you know it," he softly scolded her.

"Do I?" she turned in his arms to pin him with a questioning glare filled with hope, filled with doubt.

He decided on a different tactic. "This all started because you're worried about pregnancy. We don't even know if you're pregnant." Yet. He felt terrible because she so obviously didn't want it, but every fiber of his being hoped she was. God, the idea of finally having a child. *Their* child. It nearly sent him to his knees.

She snorted. "How many of the Impulse pairs have conceived from first consummation?"

Jericho hesitated. "There have been only two of us—"

She shook her head. "How. Many."

"Both." He said the word so softly, she wouldn't have heard it if she didn't have enhanced hearing.

"That's right," she said. "One hundred percent conception rate, Jericho."

"So, let me show you how it will be different, sweetheart," he begged. "Let me marry you. Make a family with you. If you're pregnant, I'll be over the moon. We'll be happy."

She was shaking her head, and his words drifted off. She gave him a sad smile. "Show me how it will be different? Every man in my life has said some variation of what you just told me. How many of them do you see around now?"

"Me," he said, gulping down panic. "I'm around."

A frantic pounding came from the bedroom door. "Dahlia!" a woman screamed.

They both froze, fear stealing through Jericho's veins like poison.

Dahlia burst into action, swooping down, grabbing Jericho's

pants and tossing them to him. He quickly stepped into them as Dahlia opened the door.

Esperanza burst into the room. Frantic Spanish poured from her mouth as she clung desperately to Dahlia's arms. Jericho could understand nothing of what was being said, but he knew from the woman's tone that something terrible had happened.

Dahlia leaned in closer, and Jericho could see her focusing on Esperanza's words, and then her face blanched. Her knees gave out, and Jericho rushed forward and caught her just before she hit the floor.

"What is it?" he demanded.

"He's gone," she moaned.

Jericho's heart stopped. She didn't have to tell him who "he" was. Gabriel was missing.

He switched over into soldier-mode with his next heartbeat. "When?" It had to have been recently. Jericho realized with a start that Gabriel had been taken while he and Dahlia were closed up in this room together. He'd distracted her, and as a result, her son had been taken.

He groaned. He had to make this right. She had every right to hate him, but he was going to do what he could to make it up to her.

And that meant getting Gabriel back and making sure he was never in danger again.

Both women were inconsolable. "When?" Jericho asked again, this time firmer. Dahlia's head snapped up at his tone, and he was relieved to see that, instead of anger, determination shone on her face.

"Just now," she said. "From the front yard where he was . . . playing." Her voice broke on the last word.

He nodded once. "Okay, I need weapons." He already knew where Dahlia's stash was, but she didn't know that. Rather than distract her anymore, he chose to let her lead him to the hidden gun safe below the floorboards in the corner of the room.

Esperanza's sobs provided a soundtrack for them as Jericho picked through the guns, appreciative for Dahlia's good taste. He picked up two matching Sig Sauers and a shoulder holster. Dahlia surprised him when she picked up a knife in an ankle sheath and a modified Beretta, which she stuffed into the back of her pants.

He shot her a questioning glance, which she returned with grim determination. "You're going to get him, right?" she asked. When he nodded, she said, "Then, I'm coming with you."

Relief that his Dahlia—the strong, kick-ass fighter—was back filled his chest, and he couldn't resist pulling her in for a brief hug. "I'll fix this," he said.

Her eyes flashed doubt, but she nodded. They walked to the door, where Dahlia paused briefly to whisper to Esperanza in Spanish. The older woman, who looked like she'd aged decades in the last few minutes, nodded and whispered, *"Mi hijo es malo. Matenlo."*

Dahlia drew back sharply. After a couple of tense seconds, she nodded, then looked at Jericho, motioning for him to lead the way.

He walked out of the room, down the hallway, and out of the house with Dahlia fast on his heels. "What did she say?" he asked as they both climbed into the truck.

She looked at him briefly, and then directed her eyes forward. "She said her son is evil. And to kill him."

Jericho turned in his seat, looked out the back window, and reversed out of the driveway. It would not be hard to follow this son of a bitch. The neighbors stood in their yards gazing down the road in the direction he had gone.

Chapter Fifteen

Dahlia stared in the direction her neighbors were looking. Nothing slipped by in this neighborhood. But Dahlia was shocked that her neighbors were not only out on the street, but obviously waving them on in the direction Luis had taken Gabriel.

Usually when something like this happened, everyone stayed inside, away from the doors and windows.

But then again, nothing like this had ever really happened before. There was an unspoken agreement among rivals that children were off-limits. Now that that agreement had been broken, it appeared the neighborhood was ready to break its silence.

Jericho drove dangerously fast, and they were out of the neighborhood in seconds. Suddenly, there were no neighbors to guide them. Panic rose in Dahlia's throat again.

"How will we know where he is?" she asked Jericho desperately.

Without taking his eyes from the road, Jericho reached behind his seat and fished around. Seconds later, his hand emerged clutching some sort of device. He tossed it her direction and returned both hands to the wheel.

Dahlia recognized it as soon as she got her hands on it. "A tracking device?"

He eyed her warily before saying, "I've put one on him, and you, every day."

She was speechless. He reached toward her, shoved aside her hair, and plucked something from the back of her shirt. He held it before her face. It was a little metal disc, about the size of a dime, covered in what looked like Velcro hooks.

"You were a flight risk," he said apologetically.

Dahlia closed her eyes and breathed deeply for the first time since she'd discovered her son was taken. "Oh, thank God," she breathed.

The relief she felt she saw echoed in Jericho's features. No, he wasn't going to get in trouble for this. It was going to save her son.

Without another word, she flipped open the device. It was one she was familiar with from her military training. She nearly cried with joy when she saw the blip on the radar. Her husband wouldn't have thought to search the small boy for tracking devices.

"It looks like they're about five miles ahead of us."

Jericho said nothing, but stepped on the gas. The truck lurched forward, and Dahlia grabbed for the "Oh Jesus" handle. She held on with all her might and thanked God that Jericho was a genius behind the wheel and handling the enormous truck with ease. He wove in and out of traffic effortlessly.

"Don't worry," he said to her loudly over the roar of the engine. "We'll get him back."

Her eyes stung with unshed tears. His help meant more to her than anything in the world.

They covered ground quickly, and then the blip stopped moving. "They've stopped," Dahlia shouted. Her heart thudded. "I know the place. An abandoned factory."

Luis had taken their son to where they had all hung out when they were young and stupid. She couldn't believe the building was still standing. It had been an utter pile of shit back when she'd been a teenager and stupid in love with the older, wiser—or so she'd thought—Luis. He had to be pretty confident that he'd get away with it to take Gabriel there. There wasn't even any place to hide.

A muscle ticked in Jericho's cheek. He didn't take his eyes off the road, but his hand left the wheel and landed on her thigh, where he squeezed reassuringly. "We'll get Gabriel back, sweetheart. I promise you."

She nodded and gestured to the side of the road. "Pull over here. The lot's close."

Jericho did as she directed, and as soon as the truck wasn't moving, Dalia was out and jogging through the dirt to the lot around the corner. Jericho caught up with her quickly. Once the building was in sight, Dahlia ducked behind an old, beat-up couch. Jericho skidded to a stop beside her. They breathed heavily from the run, but both of them made sure not to make a sound.

While they waited to catch their breath, Dahlia took in the scene. Not much had changed in the last decade. The lot was still surrounded by a derelict chain-link fence that was down in many areas. Stolen furniture spotted the front, barren lawn, and the tall, gray building rose up into the night sky. Most of the windows were gone, allowing an uninhibited view of the abandoned inside. But in the bottom floor, a trashcan fire was clearly visible, sending nightmarish shadows to the walls.

The night's silence was rent by the sound of a small boy's cries, and Dahlia stiffened and prepared to spring to her feet. Jericho grabbed her arm and squeezed. It was a small movement, but it brought her back to earth.

"Listen," he hissed at her. "Those aren't cries of pain."

Dahlia forced herself to breathe in slowly through her nose and actually listened to her son cry. Jericho was right. Gabriel was scared, but those weren't the anguished cries of pain.

"Anything I should know about on the first floor before we go in?" he asked in a whisper.

Dahlia shook her head. "Nothing. It's a wide open room."

Jericho grunted. "No cover."

She watched as he thought for a few seconds.

"Put up your weapon," Jericho softly ordered, and Dahlia realized that she'd palmed her gun. When had that happened? She silently returned it to the back of her pants. "You stay behind me, you got it?" he told her, and then before she could make sense of his words, he stood up calmly and walked toward the gaping threshold.

Dahlia scrambled to her feet and moved after him, making sure to stay behind him like he'd ordered. She didn't want him distracted by trying to keep her safe if she forced the issue and strode in next to him.

Jericho entered the building. He reached behind him and snagged Dahlia at the waist and jerked her into his back as he walked. She bumped into him, and her feet tangled with his, but he didn't slow down. "Stay close," he whispered.

Gabriel's cries were overshadowed by three adult male voices. Dahlia's eyes adjusted to the dark, and she peered around Jericho's body as they walked. She could make out the shadows surrounding the trashcan in the far corner of the room. Gabriel was huddled on the floor between two tall men, and the form of her husband was kneeling before Gabriel. He was speaking to the boy in a low voice that Dahlia couldn't make out, and then she saw him reach forward to touch her son's shoulder, and Dahlia lost it.

She shoved Jericho aside, reaching for her gun at the same time. She kicked something that rattled and all three men turned as one and drew their weapons. Dahlia didn't care, she just continued to charge forward, aiming directly for Luis. "Don't touch my son," she growled.

Gabriel heard her voice. His little head jerked up and then he scrambled to his feet. "*Mamá!*" he screamed as he surged forward.

Luis snatched him by the back of his shirt and dragged him back against his body, and Dahlia froze.

"*Your* son?" Luis asked in a deadly calm. Dahlia knew what was coming next. That was always the tone of voice he used right before he hit her. Her gun hand wavered. Luis cocked his head like a dog and stared her down cruelly. "*Your son?*" he bellowed.

Dahlia whimpered. "Luis, please," she breathed, just as she had so many times.

"This is *my* son, bitch. You tried to keep him from me, and now you'll never see him again." He laughed and chills ran down Dahlia's back. "Tried to keep the existence of my own son from me."

Suddenly, Jericho's warmth met her back. One of his hands

came to rest on her shoulder, and she was reminded that she wasn't alone. Her gun hand stopped shaking.

"We've called the police," Jericho said the lie softly, smoothly. "They'll be here any minute. You can't win. Why don't you just send the boy over here?"

The gun that had been at Luis's side jerked up. He waved it around wildly. "Who the *fuck* is this?" he screamed.

Dahlia winced. He was so angry. He had his arm around her son. She started to shake again.

"Easy," Jericho said, raising both his hands up in a non-threatening manner and stepping around Dahlia, putting himself between her and Luis's gun. "I'm nobody, okay? We just want Gabriel back."

"You fucking my wife?" Luis asked. Then he snorted. "Good riddance. She was a lousy lay anyway."

Jericho growled and took a step forward. "Talk about her that way again, and I'll tear your throat out."

*

Jericho took two steps forward to do just that. No one did this to his family. The sound of a gun being cocked rent the night air, and Jericho froze in front of Dahlia. Luis had placed the barrel of his gun against Gabriel's head. Dahlia groaned and grabbed onto Jericho's arms to keep from slipping to the floor. Gabriel started crying again.

"If the police are coming, then what do I have to lose?" Luis asked, desperation coloring his voice. "If I can't have him, no one can."

Jericho immediately realized he'd underestimated the evil this man was capable of. If Jericho didn't do something, he was going to watch Gabriel die. The thought scared him worse than anything he'd experienced in years.

"Drop the gun," Jericho ordered. His hands itched for his own weapon.

Luis laughed. "Fuck no." He nodded to the two men on either side of him. "I'll kill the boy, and then we'll kill—"

Jericho didn't even have time to think, to ponder that his next step was going to single-handedly ensure that Dahlia didn't need him for protection ever again. He had no time to think about all he was about to lose. He simply breathed, jerked, and had a gun in each hand. Two shots sounded and Luis and the man to his right went down. The remaining man fumbled to cock his gun and before Luis even hit the ground, Jericho had taken him out, too.

Gabriel was left standing among three bodies.

Dahlia surged forward and reached her son in seconds, scooping him up and pressing his face into her neck where he sobbed his heart out, his little body wracked with shakes. "Don't look, baby," she whispered to him as she didn't follow her own advice. Her eyes were plastered to Luis's body and the perfect hole in the center of his forehead. Without looking at the others, Jericho knew that they were all perfect shots. Shots that had saved Gabriel's life and freed Dahlia from Luis's reign of terror forever.

Jericho's arms came around them both. "Shh," he whispered. "It's over."

Dahlia's knees gave out. Jericho caught her, and swung her up into his arms, even though she still held Gabriel. He held both of them securely, shifting Dahlia's body until Gabriel was safely nestled against her stomach, and then Jericho turned and began the walk back to the truck.

Dahlia clutched her son as close as she could and turned her head to sob into Jericho's chest.

Jericho's heart still pounded through his chest. His instinct was screaming at him to get his family out of this situation as fast as possible, and so he nearly tripped over his feet as he walked as fast as he could without alarming the already distraught bundle of people in his arms.

He'd almost lost Gabriel. Forever. The boy was vulnerable and unchanged. A bullet from that gun would have ended his life.

And watching that fucking lunatic point a gun at his woman—rational thought had left him. He still wasn't entirely aware of everything that had gone down in that factory. He just knew that he'd handled the situation. The three men who had set out to hurt what was his were dead, and now Jericho was taking the two most important people in his life to safety.

End of story.

Dahlia and Gabriel would not be coming home with him; they wouldn't need to. Jericho had just changed his life forever, had lost the love of his life for the second time, and it was all worth it. He'd do it again in a heartbeat. His suffering meant nothing next to the potential for theirs.

He arrived at the truck and gently settled Dahlia and Gabriel into the passenger side. He shut the door, and then he sprinted around the front of the truck, uncomfortable being away from them for even the short amount of time it took him to reach the driver's side. A thought that brought to quick relief what he would be facing as soon as he left them. He wrenched open the door, slid into the seat, and immediately reached for them both, pulling them into his side. He took a brief moment to press them to his chest in an embrace, and then pulled back, keeping one arm around Dahlia's shoulders, so he could start the truck and get them the hell out of here before someone called the police for real.

He pulled onto the road at the same time that Dahlia curled into him further, burying her face in his chest and smashing the small boy against his ribs. Jericho could feel Gabriel squirm, and joy shot through his chest again that the boy was alive and well. He gave Dahlia a firm squeeze and just let her rely on him for warmth and security.

The trip back to the house took much longer than Jericho had patience for. He wanted to return them to their home, tuck them safely in bed, and watch over them as they slept. He wanted them to wake up together the next morning as a family. Do normal things like walk Gabriel to school, cook dinner, have family game night. He wanted that with them so bad.

He could never have it.

Jericho drove slowly down the street to the house. All of the neighbors had returned to the indoors. The neighborhood looked like a ghost town compared to what it'd been when they'd left earlier.

Jericho breathed a sigh of relief that he almost had them home. He followed the track of the headlights as he turned into the driveway, and then slammed on the brakes as the beams illuminated someone leaning against a strange, official-looking car.

Eli Johnson was waiting for him in the driveway.

Chapter Sixteen

"Shit," Jericho whispered before he could stop himself.

Dahlia stiffened against him and raised her head. As soon as she saw Eli, she jerked and pulled Gabriel into the shield of her body even further. "No," she moaned. "This isn't happening." Frantic eyes found Jericho. "I can't lose my son," she whispered to him.

Jericho closed his eyes against the raw pain he saw in Dahlia's features. This was all his fault. He'd dragged his feet in his mission, and now his mission had come to him. Of course, they were able to find him. He was a moron. He'd been using his cellphone like some kind of freaking green idiot.

Eli was here for Dahlia. Since Jericho had failed to bring her back into headquarters, Eli would.

Jericho couldn't let that happen. "You won't lose him," he said, opening his eyes and solemnly promising Dahlia. "I'll handle this. Take Gabriel and go inside."

Jericho opened the driver's side door and hopped to the pavement. He helped Dahlia slide over and lifted her and the boy to the ground. He then pivoted, placing himself between one of his dearest friends and the woman he loved, and helped escort them to the walkway. Once they reached Eli, Jericho let them go into the house alone and turned to face his friend.

Eli looked like he'd been slapped in the head with a beam. "Was that a . . . *child*?"

Jericho stopped right before him and ignored the question. "You're not taking her back."

A grim frown marred Eli's face. "Jericho—" he began.

Jericho stepped forward, into Eli's personal space, purposefully straightening to his full height, which was several inches above Eli's. "You're *not taking her*," he said in almost a whisper.

Eli flinched. "What the fuck's happened to you? She's a murderer! She goes back to the base or she goes to prison."

Jericho surprised himself when he snarled. His hand came up to fist Eli's shirt, and he snatched his friend close until their noses were almost brushing. "She's a mother. And my mate. That matters more. You threaten her happiness one more time, and I will kill you. As many times as I need to until you come to grips with it."

Some unidentifiable emotion snapped in Eli's eyes. His features relaxed, though his expression turned sad. "You're in love with her."

It wasn't a question, but Jericho gave a jerky nod nonetheless.

"Shit," Eli breathed. He then looked down to where Jericho's hand was fisted in his shirt. "You wanna let go of me so we can talk?" he asked.

Jericho frowned. Not what he expected. He released Eli, who sank back down on his heels and took a step back, rolling his shoulders. "I'm not your enemy," Eli whispered shortly, and Jericho felt shame again, but quickly pushed it aside. If he was planning on taking Dahlia away from Gabriel, then he was the enemy. He just didn't realize it.

"You can't take her away from her son, Eli. He needs her."

Eli looked behind him at the dilapidated house where Dahlia and her son lived. "She was hiding a son." He shook his head. "I would have never guessed it."

"She was protecting him against the boy's father," Jericho said. "That's no longer an issue, but Gabriel still needs Dahlia around. And she needs him. He's her life."

Eli's eyes snapped back to Jericho. "No longer an issue?" he asked. "Jericho, what's going on here?"

Jericho shrugged apologetically.

"Christ, you didn't kill a civilian, did you?"

Jericho crossed his arms over his chest.

"No, he didn't kill a civilian," Dahlia said from right beside him, causing Jericho to jump. He had no idea how long she'd been out here. "He killed an ex-con with a gun to a child's head."

Jericho turned to her, again placing himself between her and Eli. "You don't have to say anything. I'll handle it."

"You're not doing a very good job," she said candidly. "He's freaking out that you've gone crazy." She dodged around Jericho. "Am I right?" she asked Eli.

Eli nodded. "Well, yeah," he said as though it were obvious.

Dahlia took a big breath. "I took the job with Major Taylor because he promised to help me keep my son's existence from his father, Luis. I got word that Luis found out about Gabriel, and so I left the facility the only way I could. Jericho found me and has been helping me keep Gabriel safe. Tonight, Luis kidnapped Gabriel and threatened to kill him. Jericho only killed Luis when he had no other choice."

Some of this had been news to Jericho as well. "Taylor was helping you protect Gabriel?" he asked.

Dahlia turned her soulful brown eyes on him. "Why else do you think I would work for him?" Jericho noticed that Eli was watching her very closely.

"You're lying," Eli said, his voice rough.

Jericho bristled. "Now wait a minute." Suddenly, he had an idea. He reached forward and snagged Dahlia's hand. Immediately, the Knowledge whispered *good* to him. "Ask her whatever you want," he told Eli. "I'll tell you if she's lying."

Eli's eyes widened. "Fine." He rounded on Dahlia. "How many people have you killed?"

Jericho's heart stopped beating as he watched Dahlia's face. He didn't want to hear this. Dahlia nervously shifted her weight.

"Answer the question," Eli snapped. "How many lives have you personally ended?"

Dahlia's eyes grew steely. "None, okay?" She took a deep breath. "I haven't *personally* killed anyone, but that doesn't mean I'm not guilty of killing. I let Taylor do . . . horrible things," her voice broke, and she stopped talking and closed her eyes.

The Knowledge whispered *good*. Jericho turned slightly toward Eli. "Truth," he said softly. He squeezed Dahlia's hand, and she opened her eyes. Anguish filled her face, and tears swam at the brim of her lashes. "How many experiments did you conduct with Taylor?" Jericho asked her gently.

"Also none," she said on a shuddering breath. "It was my job to get the women out of the facility whenever it was time for an experiment."

Eli sucked in a loud breath and looked at Jericho desperately. "Also truth," Jericho confirmed after listening for the Knowledge.

Eli's fists clenched and unclenched by his sides. "Are you good or evil?" he asked, confusion clearly marking his face.

Dahlia shut her eyes. "I don't . . . know," she finally whispered after several seconds.

And Jericho could stand it no longer. He tugged her forward by her hand until she collided with his chest, and then he wrapped both arms around her. He shot Eli a dirty look over her head and leaned in to whisper in her ear. "You're good, sweetheart. Never doubt that." He loved her so much in that moment. He couldn't ever imagine loving her more. "You listen to me," Jericho said to Eli. "She's done nothing to you personally. You have no reason to seek revenge from her anymore. Everything she did she did to protect her son. She's just as much a victim as you are. That little boy in there needs her. You have to let her—let this—go."

Eli closed his eyes, and Jericho watched him take a deep breath. He held it for several seconds, and then blew it out and opened his eyes. "I love you, brother," he told Jericho. "If this means that much to you, we'll figure something out. I don't know what we can do, but I couldn't stand for something to separate us."

Jericho swallowed around the lump in his throat, silently thanking God that he didn't have to say goodbye to his woman and his best friend in the same night. He reached out his right hand and offered it to Eli, who quickly grasped it and gave it a firm squeeze.

Suddenly, Eli frowned. He pulled his hand away and stared at the palm. He jerked his head up. "You're bleeding," he said, laying his palm flat and showing Jericho the smear of blood that marred its surface.

Dahlia jerked away from him at the words, and they both looked at Eli's hand. Then Dahlia grabbed Jericho's hand and raised it up to catch the dim light coming from the street lamps.

Light splashed across his skin, illuminating a deep cut on his index finger.

Jericho frowned. He didn't remember getting it.

"Is that from . . . ," Dahlia seemed to be choosing her words carefully, "the sword we found?"

Something began to tingle in the back of Jericho's neck. "No, it can't be. That would have healed by now."

"You cut yourself on the sword?" Eli asked anxiously.

"It was just a nick, Eli," Jericho replied, for some reason feeling like he was in trouble and had to explain himself.

Eli's face grew grim.

"What's going on?" Jericho asked.

"We've been working off of Taylor's theory," Eli said hesitantly. "So far, we think he's right: the sword might be the only thing that can kill someone who's eaten the fruit from the Tree of Eternal Life."

Dahlia gasped. "Is Jericho going to be okay?" she demanded.

Eli lifted his hand up in surrender. "It's still a theory. We've called in a language expert to translate whatever is written on the sword. We'll know more after she takes a look at it."

"And until then?" Jericho heard himself whisper. He couldn't help thinking that this was something he deserved after his recent behavior.

"I really think you'll be fine," Eli whispered back. "We'll keep an eye on it. It's just a scratch, not a mortal wound."

He didn't look convinced. Jericho swallowed.

"When can we expect you back at the compound?" Eli asked Jericho after several seconds of tense silence.

Jericho looked at Dahlia out of the corner of his eye, wondering how she would respond to the question.

She blanched, and Jericho felt his heart fall to his feet and shatter. This was where it all ended.

"I'm not . . . I can't . . . ." Dahlia shook her head in horror, misunderstanding the "you" to encompass both Jericho and herself.

Eli's eyes widened briefly, and he cast Jericho a look. "I'll just go sit in the car for a while." And then he turned on his heel and beat a hasty retreat.

With leaden feet, Jericho turned toward Dahlia. "Won't you come with me?" he couldn't stop himself from asking.

She closed her eyes, for all the world appearing as though she were in mortal pain.

Words continued to pour from his mouth. "I can make a home for you and Gabriel. We'll live off base. Please—" his voice broke on the word, and Dahlia held up a hand.

"Stop," she barely whispered. "Jericho, I can't stand anymore. You have to stop."

Jericho snapped his mouth shut, swallowing the remainder of his heart and soul and bracing himself for the worst.

*

Dahlia took a deep breath. She was stalling, praying for the strength she would need to tell him no when everything in her heart demanded that she say yes.

All that he'd offered sounded so wonderful. She could have Gabriel *and* Jericho. He would keep her safe. They could start a family together. Unconsciously, Dahlia's hand came to rest on her lower stomach. She could be growing their child right now— probably was.

That snapped her to attention. "No," she whispered. Not just no, but hell no. There was no way she was going to get pulled into a relationship with a man because she was carrying his baby. That did not make a happy relationship.

And everything Jericho had offered *did* seem wonderful. In fact, so wonderful that she would come to rely on him—as she had already started to do in the last few days. He would suck her in, and before she knew it, she would be right back where she was now: recovering from the devastating life choice of choosing to love the wrong man. For all of the wrong reasons.

A baby. A compulsory love. That was no reason to be with someone.

And so she had to be strong.

She closed her eyes. "I'm not going with you," she whispered.

Even though he had to have been expecting it, she heard his breath catch, and thought she also heard a soft groan of pain.

She brought her eyes to his, but immediately closed them against the sight of tears brimming in the bottom of his eyes.

"Do you . . . love me?" he asked.

She did. She loved him with all her heart. Just as she'd loved Gabriel's father before everything went to hell. What was to prevent Jericho from doing exactly what Luis had done? "It doesn't matter," Dahlia told him.

"It matters to me," Jericho said through gritted teeth as one tear slipped from his lower eyelid and trailed down his cheek.

She realized he would never let her go if she told him she loved him, so she did what she had to. "No," she nearly choked around the lie. "I don't love you."

He reached for her hand, but she jerked it out of the way.

"Believe what I'm telling you," she whispered viciously. "Believe what I'm saying without proof. No one in my life has ever trusted me, not even when it comes to matters of my own heart."

Jericho's hand dropped back to his side. His sigh was one of utter defeat, and Dahlia knew with sickening certainty that she had won. She had succeeded in driving him away. She hoped he left soon, because she had perhaps two minutes before she broke down into sobs.

"I'll always love you, Dahlia," he whispered to the pavement at his feet. "And if the only way I can show you that is to give you your freedom, then so be it. But know that I will always be waiting for you."

Without another look or word, he turned away from her and strode to Eli's waiting vehicle. Dahlia watched through her wavering tears as he drove out of her life.

*

Jericho was reminded once more why Eli was his best friend when he didn't demand any answers but simply drove them away from Dahlia's house as quickly as possible.

In the quiet of the SUV cab, Jericho struggled for control. Every mile that separated him from his mate was excruciating. He wasn't sure how he was keeping himself from utterly breaking down or bellowing out his pain and startling Eli into crashing the car. He had to make a noise or explode, so he forced himself to talk to his friend. "How are we . . . going . . . to explain . . . ." That was as far as Jericho could get. Complex thought was beyond him at this moment. He only knew that he'd royally screwed things up for Eli. Now Eli had a missing prisoner to explain because of his loyalty to Jericho.

"The sword," Eli said simply, somehow knowing what Jericho was getting at. "When you retrieved the sword, she was there at the facility. You fought, and she took a mortal blow."

Jericho shivered at the finality of Eli's plan. If they spread the rumor that Dahlia was dead, what were the chances that he would ever be able to get her back? "I can't . . . tell that to people," he murmured. Pain kicked in his chest at the thought of Dahlia dead.

"I understand. I wouldn't be able to either if it was Abilene," Eli said. "We'll write the statement together. You'll sign it. The case will be closed. You won't be questioned. I'll let them know it would be too painful for you to discuss the death of your mate."

Jericho couldn't figure out why Eli was being so kind to him. This whole plan was going to blow up in their faces, and for what? So Jericho could live in misery away from his woman so she could be free? No one in this car was benefiting from that.

Still. "Thank you," Jericho whispered hoarsely. It was the best option they had.

Chapter Seventeen

Three months later

Dahlia glared at the pair of movers standing on her front porch. "You want to repeat that again?" she asked them in a tone of voice that suggested their answer had better be no.

The two men glanced nervously at each other, and then one of them said, "We're here to move your things to your new house."

Dahlia blinked once. Twice. She pursed her lips. "I wasn't aware that I was moving. Or that I had a new house."

Both men frowned. "We've never heard that before," one of them said hesitantly.

The other one lost his patience. "Look, lady. Here's the order. It was placed last week. You're paid in full, and we're to take your items across town to this address." He showed Dahlia the paperwork and pointed with a grubby finger at an address.

Dahlia took a stumbling step back. That address was in the wealthy part of town. Her heart sank.

This was Jericho's doing. Again.

She looked over her shoulder to the interior of the house, taking in the high-end furniture that had been arriving weekly since Dahlia had sent Jericho away. Another new car—a sporty BMW for Esperanza—sat beside the truck Jericho had purchased in the driveway, and she could hear Gabriel shouting at the television as he played video games on his shiny new PlayStation.

Frustration boiled up inside of her. Even though she'd sent him away, he was still finding ways to be in her life—to make her rely on him. And he'd been devious in the timing of the gifts by waiting until Gabriel would be home from school so he would see them. And she wasn't the type of mother who would snatch a better way of living from her child's hands just because she resented the giver.

But a house? There was only one explanation for the progressively extravagant gifts. Jericho knew.

Dahlia felt a flare of panic. "No, this isn't happening. Give me the keys to the house and go away."

The one who had lost patience said, "We don't have the damn keys, lady. It's *your* house. You're supposed to have the keys."

The last of Dahlia's temper ignited. "Go! Get back in your truck and go." They seemed startled, but turned to do so. "Wait, give me that," she hissed, reaching out and snatching the order that contained the house's address. She didn't even watch them leave as she pulled out her new cellphone—another gift from Jericho—and did a quick Google search on the property, locating the name of the real estate company that had made the sale. She dialed the number of the main office.

As soon as the secretary answered, Dahlia said, "Yes, I'm from the gas department. There's a problem over at," she looked down at the paper in her hand, "850 Cherry Street. Nothing huge that needs immediate attention, but I can't seem to find the new purchaser's contact information. Can you contact the buyer and tell them to meet me there this evening?" It was short notice, but she knew Jericho would drop everything to come to her if she asked. And that did not make her happy. At all.

She thanked the woman as she assured her she would get the message to the new homeowner and ended the call. Her stomach gave a leap of joy that she quickly squelched. She would not be excited about seeing Jericho again. She simply had to see him face-to-face to tell him to knock off all the gifts.

That was all.

*

Jericho slammed down the phone in the main room of the facility, causing everyone to swing around and stare at him.

The small huddle in the middle of the room contained a ready-to-pop Abilene, a hovering Eli, several scientists, and the new addition to the facility: language expert Grace Tucker, PhD. They had been leaning over the flaming sword doing God-knows-what—just as they'd been doing for the last three months—until Jericho's uncharacteristic display of exuberance distracted them.

He couldn't keep his idiot smile from his face, and Eli tilted his head as he observed him. A concerned expression crossed his face, and he leaned down to kiss Abilene's head quickly, then gestured for Jericho to follow him into Eli's office.

As soon as the door was closed, Eli pounced. "She contacted you didn't she?"

Jericho nodded and then shook his head. "Well, not directly. But I'm going to be seeing her tonight." He thought his heart was going to crack from being too full as he thought about finally seeing her face again. Holding her. Kissing her. Loving her.

Eli sighed resignedly. "Do whatchya gotta do, man. God, I don't know how I'm going to explain how she didn't die to everyone if you bring her back."

Even the possibility had his grin widening. He ran to his room to pack. Two hours later he was at the airport, and a quick five-hour flight later, he was back in Southern California driving his rental car to the address of the house he'd purchased for Dahlia, Gabriel, and Esperanza.

She was waiting for him when he got there. The truck he'd bought sat in the driveway, and she was sitting on the porch swing, pushing back and forth agitatedly. When she spotted him pulling up to the curb, she launched from her seat and stormed in his direction.

And all of Jericho's hope fizzled. Shit. He wasn't here because she wanted him; he was here because he was in trouble.

How was he going to go back to his life after this? After seeing her again? After the hope he'd had that they would finally be together?

His legs weighed hundreds of pounds as he forced himself to leave the cocoon of his car, still perfumed with hope. He took one step onto the lawn, and she pitched something at him. He caught it instinctively right before it hit his chest, and then he opened his palm.

Keys. If he had one guess, he would say keys to her new house that he'd had left for her in her new mailbox.

"I know you know, Jericho, so cut the shit," she yelled on a huff.

Jericho froze. What was it that he knew? Possibilities flew through Jericho's mind. Did she have a man? His heart plummeted. "Where is he?" Jericho forced himself to ask. God help him, if this man wasn't worthy of Dahlia, Jericho was going to—what? Kill him. He didn't laugh at the thought, which only worried him more.

"Gabriel isn't here," she snapped.

"I'm not talking about Gabriel, and you know it," he said softly.

"I don't know if it's a boy yet, Jericho. God."

Jericho's knees felt wobbly. Had he heard that right? Could the thing he was supposed to know all about be a baby? "Dahlia," he began, licking his suddenly dry lips. "Sweetheart, are you . . . pregnant?"

She froze like a deer in the headlights. "Oh God," she said and closed her eyes. "You didn't know." They were silent for several seconds, each embroiled in their own thoughts, and then she opened her eyes. "You didn't know?"

Jericho managed to nod once, and then he fell to his knees, clutched Dahlia's hips and dragged her forward so he could bury his face in her stomach. "My baby," he whispered against her, not sure which of the beings he currently held he was talking about.

He felt her fingers in his hair, and he rubbed his face back and forth against Dahlia's dress, thrilled at the slight bulge he felt there.

"If you didn't know, why did you send—" She drifted off.

He drew back from her warmth and smiled up at her radiantly.

"I wanted you to be happy. I couldn't be here with you to make sure that happened, so I did the only thing I could. I tried to make life easier for you."

She stared at him for several long seconds, and then gave him a wavery smile. "You really love me don't you?" she asked as though she couldn't believe it.

Jericho frowned. "Of course I do," he scolded. He'd made that more than clear.

Dahlia burst into tears.

*

Oh God, how was she supposed to handle this? He was so good. Good to her. Good to her son. Just plain good.

Who spends millions of dollars on someone to make their life easier? Things like that just don't happen.

She covered her face with her hands and let her sobs overtake her. She was such an idiot. She'd sent this man away, and he had done the only thing he could think of to make sure she knew he still loved her. She'd thrown the knowledge of their baby at him, fully expecting him to erupt in the anger and fury that Luis had when he'd found out about Gabriel.

And he'd done the one thing she hadn't anticipated: fallen to his knees at her feet and pressed his face to her womb, shuddering like she'd given him—the man who had showered her with gifts—the most precious gift in the world.

She felt the change in the air around her as Jericho rose unsteadily to his feet. His arms came around her, and he pulled her gently against him. "Shh, sweetheart," he whispered. "Your tears kill me. Please don't cry."

Which, of course, only made her cry harder.

"I love you," she said between gulping sobs, her words muffled by her hands.

She felt Jericho stiffen against her. Her hands were tugged away from her face, and his vivid blue eyes came into her vision. "What did you say?" he asked breathlessly.

She took another deep breath, calmed her nerves, and clearly stated, "I love you. So much."

And, of course, he responded in the one way that would cause her heart to melt even more. A huge grin split his face. He lunged at her, wrapping his arms around her and spinning her around. A barrage of kisses rained down on her face, each one peppered with a hurried, desperate "I love you," until Dahlia was laughing like a carefree child.

Suddenly, Jericho reached down, swooped up the keys he'd dropped in the yard, swept her up in his arms and made for the front door of the house like a man possessed.

"Where are we going?" she asked with an uncharacteristic giggle.

"We're going to initiate every damn room in this house, sweetheart."

She tossed her head back with a laugh, her hair blowing in the wind. "Sounds like a pl—"

He cut off her last word with a searing kiss, his tongue invading her mouth. She had no idea how he could see where he was going, but she sure as hell wasn't going to open her eyes to make sure he didn't trip.

She heard him fumble with the front door, and then the crash it made as he slammed it behind them.

They never made it beyond the foyer.

About the Author

Micah Persell holds a bachelor's degree in English and a double master's degree in literature and English pedagogy. She is an avid reader of all types of literature, but has a soft spot for romance. She currently teaches high school language arts classes in California where she lives with her husband, two dogs, and two cats. *Of the Knowledge of Good and Evil* is her second book. She loves to answer e-mails and connect with readers on Facebook, Twitter, and Pinterest. Visit her website at *www.micahpersell.com*.

In the mood for more Crimson Romance? Check out *Love's Prey* by Envy Augustine at *CrimsonRomance.com*.

www.ingramcontent.com/pod-product-compliance
Lightning Source LLC
Chambersburg PA
CBHW010640100726
47900CB00011B/2915